2/23

Hayner PLD/Large Print
Overdues .10/day. Max fine cost of item. Lost or damaged item: additional $5 service charge.

MAIL-ORDER BRIDES OF THE WEST
HEATHER

Center Point
Large Print

Also by Caroline Fyffe and available from Center Point Large Print:

Heart of Eden
True Heart's Desire
Heart of Mine
An American Duchess
Heart of Dreams
Montana Dawn
Texas Twilight
Mail-Order Brides of the West: Evie

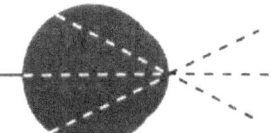

**This Large Print Book carries the
Seal of Approval of N.A.V.H.**

Mail-Order Brides of the West
Heather

A McCutcheon Family Novel
Book Four

CAROLINE FYFFE

Center Point Large Print
Thorndike, Maine

This Center Point Large Print edition
is published in the year 2023 by arrangement with
the author.

Copyright © 2013 by Caroline Fyffe.

All rights reserved.

Mail-Order Brides of The West: Heather is a work of fiction. Names, characters, places, and incidents are either products of the author's imagination or used fictitiously. Any resemblance to actual events, locales, or persons, living or dead, is wholly coincidental.

The text of this Large Print edition is unabridged.
In other aspects, this book may vary
from the original edition.
Printed in the United States of America
on permanent paper sourced using
environmentally responsible foresting methods.
Set in 16-point Times New Roman type.

ISBN: 978-1-63808-592-8

The Library of Congress has cataloged this record under
Library of Congress Control Number: 2022946073

*Dedicated to my dear sister,
Mary Turner,
with love.*

Mail-Order Brides of the West
Heather

Chapter One

St. Louis, Missouri, 1886

Oh, for heaven's sake! Heather Stanford swatted at a fly buzzing about her face and blew a wayward strand of hair from her eyes before it stuck to her moist forehead. Although they stood in the shade, the temperature was warm and growing hotter.

Heather glanced from beneath her lashes at the group gathered in the backyard. All the bride hopefuls were there listening to Mr. De Rosa teach them about planting seasons, when to put in herbs for your kitchen garden, and how to keep pesky critters—Heather swatted at a bee this time—from stealing the best of what they grew.

She nibbled at her bottom lip, thinking how the crooked little man with the pointed leather cap reminded her of a troll from the battered copy of *Grimm's Fairy Tales* she used to read to her younger sisters at bedtime. But Mr. De Rosa wasn't mean at all. He had a heart of pure gold. His eyes came alight anytime a bride hopeful asked a rare question, and a smile was never far from his lips.

Rumor had it he was sweet on Dona, the cook, but Heather had never seen proof of that.

Picturing the two of them together was difficult, him short, her tall and strong as an ox. Lina had found them face-to-face in the pantry, Dona with an expression of guilt, as if they'd been caught with their hands in the cookie jar. Heather's lips twitched.

Angelina Napolitano, or Lina as she liked to be called, nudged her when the sound of heavy iron wheels on brick and the clanging of cables was impossible to miss. "Listen. The cable car," she whispered, leaning toward Heather.

Heather tilted her head, singling out the sound amidst the chirping birds, buzzing from the honeycomb high in the alder, and Mr. De Rosa's voice droning on and on and on.

She nodded. "I hear it." St. Louis's first cable car line stopped only one street over on the corner of Knoll and Franklin. The conveyance's distinctive chugging along Franklin Avenue permeated the air, then the conductor's shrill voice called out the stop. All the girls turned, and Mr. De Rosa smiled and stopped talking. The novelty of this new mode of transportation had not worn off.

"Attention, p-please, ladies," Mr. De Rosa stuttered, calling them back to what they were doing. He held a pencil in his dirt-covered fingers. "Now, t-take the pencil and p-p-*poke* it into your prepared soil, three to f-four inches deep. Then p-p-*plaaace* your rosemary cutting inside." He went about doing just that, a little hum coming from his throat as his son, Ernie, a good twenty feet away, pruned the dwarf plum at the back of the carp pond with large hedge shears.

"Let's plan an outing when we have time, ride the cable car. Just down to Locust Street and back," Lina whispered. "We can visit the flower shop, then have a cup of tea in a charming little café. I've seen just the one. I'm dying to go."

"I don't know . . ." Heather didn't want to dampen Lina's enthusiasm, but she didn't have money to spare. Even five cents was too much.

"And it's *my* treat." As always, it seemed Lina had read her thoughts. "No argument from you. Remember, you just helped me hem that horrible skirt with yards and yards of fabric. If left to my own devices, I would have donated the garment to the church. Your stitches were much tighter and smoother than mine." She gave Heather an affectionate look. "Consider the excursion a thank-you for your kindness."

Mr. De Rosa lifted his head and gave them the stop-whispering eye and pay-attention look.

Lina was Heather's closest friend. The curvy Italian with the nurturing spirit had recognized Heather's reluctance to be a mail-order bride right off.

At twenty-six, Lina was older than Heather by four years, and for the prior eight years had been a nanny for a fine family on the East side. After her boys, as she called them, had grown up and gone off to boarding school, she didn't want to return to her crowded family home. Instead, she hoped to be a mail-order bride. She was sincere and smart, and Heather considered her the older sister she didn't have. They were roommates, along with Bertha Bucholtz, in the attic dormitory.

Kathryn Ford, the well-off socialite from Mount Vernon, inched forward. "I've never liked to work with the soil, really." She held up her perfect, made-for-playing-the-piano fingers, studied them for a moment, then clasped them behind her back.

Heather hid a smile. Her friend Kathryn was here in defiance of the man her father had picked out for her the day she was born. *Imagine that.* "A boor and domineering," Kathryn had called him one afternoon when they were talking. Heather admired the young woman's inner strength to go up against her formidable father like that, a powerful businessman in Boston. The delicate cape of Kathryn's yellow chiffon dress, one much too expensive to be worn while gardening, draped elegantly around her shoulders, accentuating the golden highlights in her wavy chestnut hair.

Heather's heart, full of love and too many regrets, twisted a little more.

She missed her family, especially her youngest sister, Melba.

The fourteen-year-old grew frailer by the day. The whole family was worried sick, and the doctors couldn't seem to figure out what was behind her deteriorating constitution. Heather clenched her eyes in frustration and willed away the fear that threatened to darken her heart.

"It's as ea-easy as that!" Mr. De Rosa smiled warmly at the group, and Heather was snapped back to the present. "And with th-that, we're finished." He set his things down, took a handkerchief from his pocket, and wiped his shiny forehead.

Darcy Russell and Bertha Bucholtz meandered toward Heather's group, joining them.

"I'm h-hot," a female voice said from behind a bush, the mimicking tone malicious.

The girls turned.

Prudence Crawford stepped out. She laughed and threw a knowing look at the good-hearted gardener as she swished her fan in front of her apple-red face. "Aren't y-y-*yooooou?*"

In that moment, Heather disliked Prudence even more than she already did. With each passing day, the woman thought up new ways to be mean and cruel. She often picked on the poor gardener, but any of them could also be her target.

"I'm a little tired," Heather said, choosing to ignore the cruel mockery. She tried to avoid

Prudence at all costs. Someday she might lose her patience and box her ears, as she'd had to do a time or two with her little brothers. "I think I'll go freshen up for supper. Won't be long before Dona rings the dinner bell." Heather smiled, even though the action felt stilted. "As you know, Dona doesn't appreciate it if we're late."

"That I do," Lina agreed. "Yesterday I thought she was going to explode as I hurried in one minute past seven. Her eyes gave me a silent dressing down that scorched me to my pantaloons." Lina winked one of her sparkling eyes.

Darcy nodded, sending tendrils of honey-brown hair waving around her face. "I guess I can't blame her, though? She takes pride in the sumptuous suppers she prepares for us. We're really quite lucky to be treated in such a manner."

Heather took in the beautiful backyard. *Yes, lucky indeed.* Mrs. Seymour, the owner of the agency, took good care of her charges. She looked after her girls as if they were her own.

Heather had been at the agency for a little over two weeks, and Mrs. Seymour had yet to call her into her office for "a talk." A talk was a *good* thing—that is if you wanted a husband. But Heather didn't. All she wanted was a way to support herself, so she could contribute to the pool of money that had kept her family's business afloat since her father's passing. Times were hard. Had always been hard for them as far back as she could remember. And now that the doctor bills . . .

All the other brides, however, did want a husband, and continually chattered about which kind they preferred. A summons to the matron's office was the news the prospective brides longed to receive. The meeting meant Mrs. Seymour had found a potential match, and the woman fit the requirements of a particular bachelor looking for a bride.

Once presented with the details of the suitor, the prospective wife-to-be had to decide whether he fit her dreams and desires as well. Then she wrote back to see if a match could be made.

"Did I tell you what Dona did to me the day after I arrived?" Bertha looked over her shoulder toward the house, as if to make sure the cook wasn't within hearing distance. The young woman's eyes danced and her full cheeks blossomed pink. Her green dress billowed out around her in the shape of a church bell, accentuating her thick waist and stout body. "I was five minutes late to the dining room because I couldn't find my fan. When I finally arrived, my plate had been removed!" Bertha blinked several times in rapid, unbelieving succession. "I had to go to bed *hungry*—just like when I was a girl."

"Really?" Kathryn looked at her, incredulous. "That seems awful harsh."

Bertha tittered and shrugged. "I suppose. But I've been ten minutes early to every meal since."

Prudence cleared her throat loudly, then waited until all eyes were on her. "I'm not surprised, Bertha," she said. "Your stomach is like a homing pigeon. It draws your feet and nose to the tiniest hint of food."

Heather couldn't believe her ears.

Bertha's smile crumpled.

"Prudence!" Heather scolded. "Say you're sorry this instant!"

The house troublemaker was up to her usual tricks. Nasty and mean were her middle names. She enjoyed making others feel bad about themselves, and she especially liked to pick on Bertha.

Prudence straightened her long, reed-thin body and patted the side of her glossy black bun. She liked to flaunt her shape, or lack of it, in front of Bertha, who was as plump as she was sweet.

Prudence's incensed gaze bored into Heather, challenging. "I will do *no* such thing, *Miss* Stanford. I haven't said anything that everyone in this room has not thought to herself."

Bertha's face flushed pinker, if that were possible, and her eyes blinked in pain. She spun and gathered the fan and bonnet she had set on a nearby chair, as if to hurry away.

Everyone else remained frozen in shocked

silence, as bees buzzed and the sun continued to shine. Heather feared Bertha might break into tears.

"You should be *ashamed* of yourself, Pru!" Lina said, stepping to Heather's side in solidarity. "I believe you enjoy hurting other people's feelings. Why are you so cruel? Now that Evie is gone, it seems Bertha is your new target."

"Don't listen to a word that comes out of Prudence's uncharitable mouth, Bertha." Heather touched the woman's shoulder. "We don't think those things about you. Prudence is just frustrated because she's been at the agency so long—with no prospect of a match. The poor woman needs our prayers and understanding." She leveled a scrutinizing gaze at Prudence. "How long have you been here, Pru?"

Prudence's sharp intake of breath sounded around the yard. Her lips curled over her teeth, and her chin jutted out like a knife. A second later, a violent trembling overtook her arms and legs and she reminded Heather of a starving dog ready to fight to keep its bone.

Heather didn't dare back down.

Lina inched closer, as did the other young women. Ernie, pruning shears at his side, watched. Seemed they'd all chosen sides, and ended up with her.

Prudence turned and stomped away.

With their tormenter gone, Darcy, Kathryn, and

Lina huddled around Bertha, drawing her into hugs of their own.

"With Mrs. Seymour away visiting Evie, Prudence thinks she has the run of the place," Darcy said. "The cook's authority has little effect on that shrew, especially since Dona hardly comes out of the kitchen to see what's going on."

A small smile crept back onto Bertha's face. The buoyant, happy spirit resurfaced in her eyes. "When Prudence started to shake, I thought she was about to pounce on you, Heather. You've made an enemy standing up to her like that."

Heather laughed. "Oh, pooh. Prudence doesn't scare me. Bullies are usually afraid of their own shadows."

Bertha took Heather's hands in her own. "Still, I want you to keep your wits about you. I don't trust Prudence one little bit."

Heather smiled, thinking how the group of women reminded her of her own sisters. Her heart gave another sad squeeze. If she married and moved west, this might be the last few days she spent with them. And what about her little sister Melba, with her failing health? What would become of her?

"If it'll make you feel better," Heather said, shoving her disturbing thoughts aside, "I'll be on the lookout at all times."

Kathryn nodded. "I think we all should. Since Trudy Bauer's marriage, Prudence has become bolder. Trudy had a calming effect on her. She'd always change the subject at just the right time."

A thoughtful acknowledgment rippled through the group of girls as they remembered their friend. Trudy's soothing force at the agency had been well appreciated, especially where Prudence was concerned. Trudy's match had been made a couple of weeks prior, and she'd traveled west to Sweetwater Springs to marry Seth Flanigan.

"I think we should all skedaddle and get ready for supper." Heather glanced around. "Supper bell will be ringing soon enough."

Heads nodded in agreement.

In the house, Heather took the handrail and started for the attic dormitory. The talk of Trudy made her think of her other friend, Evie Davenport Holcomb, the agency's longtime maid who'd sneaked away early one morning and traveled west. The girl was almost a hero around the house. Unbeknownst to Mrs. Seymour, and in search of true love, the maid had secretly taken letters that had been sent to the agency from an eligible bachelor. Without telling anyone, she began a correspondence with him, and in no time, he asked her to wed. Such a romantic story! Later, when Mrs. Seymour learned Evie's whereabouts, she packed her bags and went after her. That was over two weeks ago. Thank goodness the matron was due home tomorrow.

"Heather," a voice called.

Heather turned to find Lina hurrying up the stairs to catch up. Her friend held up the folds of the buttery-colored cotton dress so she wouldn't catch the hem with the toe of her boot. The fitted bodice and scooped neckline were beautiful, and complemented Lina's near perfect olive skin.

Lina tipped her head. "Are you all right, Heather? Seems like something is troubling you. Besides Pru, I mean."

They continued up the stairs side by side.

"I'm just worried about Melba."

"How is she?"

Last week, Heather had confided in Lina about her youngest sister's precarious health. Sharing her fears had made them a bit more bearable. "About the same. I received a letter today from Sally, my other sister. Mother is beside herself. The doctors don't have any answers."

"I'm so sorry."

They paused on the second-story landing. Lina put a hand on Heather's shoulders. "Is there anything I can do to help?"

Heather shook her head. Her brothers were already living at their uncle's house to ease the financial burden. There was talk of Sally's going to live at Aunt Tillie's.

"Maybe Mrs. Seymour will have a match for you when she returns. Several letters have arrived since she left."

"Perhaps. But . . ." Heather felt her face heat, and she turned away.

Lina stepped closer, and with a gentle touch to Heather's chin, turned her back. "But what?"

"I don't want to sound ungrateful, but—I don't want a match." Finally saying the words she'd been keeping to herself felt good.

"What?" Lina's brows drew together. "I'm confused."

Heather nodded, resigned to her plight. "The only reason I'm here is to help my family. Money is tight. Food is hard to come by. I had to talk until I was blue in the face so my mother would believe going west to get married was my greatest heart's desire—and be a mail-order bride."

"Oh, Heather, you *can't* mean that! You don't want to marry? To have a husband?"

Heather straightened. "I do mean it, Lina. I've had this notion all my life that I wouldn't marry. That maybe I'd work in the medical field in some capacity. I knew I could never afford the schooling, but I always listened and learned from my mother and our neighborhood doctor. As I got older, being the daughter of a blacksmith, there weren't many options open for me if I did want to marry. No one was beating down the door when I came of age, and the few that were, I had no interest in. I wanted more out of life than being a slave to some tavern-loving . . ."

She stopped, knowing that Lina was excited

about being a bride. She didn't want to spoil her friend's enthusiasm about getting married.

Just because Heather's father hadn't been the best husband to her mother, or father to her and her brothers and sisters, didn't mean there weren't other good, decent men out there. She had no desire to raise a family all by herself and have her man come home with beer on his breath after too many hours away, and too much money spent. Regardless of his faults, she'd loved her father. She just didn't want a husband like him. Her uncharitable thoughts kept her awake at night, along with her gnawing stomach—a heavy burden for a young girl to have.

She smiled ruefully. "This year and last, I'd hoped to find some kind of position in St. Louis that would help ease my family's plight. I wanted to remain living at home—helping my mother. Remember, I have nine brothers and sisters. I feel strongly about my three youngest sisters, Sally, Anita, and Melba finishing their educations." *Not Melba now.* She gulped at the reality of what that thought meant. "An education is the most important thing a woman can have."

The look in Lina's eyes gave her courage to go on. "But last year the smithy slowed down even more. Since my father's passing, and new smithies open, work is harder and harder for my brothers to find. Longtime clients have died off. If I go west, there will be one less person to feed, and things will be easier. If I can't help by working and bringing in an income, I can help by starting a new life somewhere else."

She shrugged and glanced away, a shiver of uncertainty running up her spine. "As hard as I tried, no one needed a doctor's assistant, or any other type of employee. I would've taken Evie's job here as maid if Mrs. Seymour hadn't filled the position so quickly with Juniper. If I truly want to help my family, finding a husband and moving out is the best thing I can do."

Lina looked skeptical. "But the other day, when we were all talking about husbands and the kind of man we wanted, you joined in."

"That's because I didn't want anyone to know how I truly felt. If the matron finds out, she may not match me up with anyone. One way or the other, seems I'm going to have a husband. I may as well accept this cross gracefully, as Mrs. Seymour likes to say."

A smile played around the corners of Lina's mouth. "You may be surprised. Marriage might agree with you. Who knows whom you'll be matched with. Tall, dark, and handsome?" She made a slight curtsy, and then pretended to slip into the arms of an imaginary suitor. She waltzed gracefully around the second-floor landing as if at a ball.

Heather couldn't stifle a small laugh. Lina and her fanciful ways could always lighten her mood.

"I don't think so. Have you forgotten about my brothers, Travis, Morgan, Ben, Peter, Curtis, and Sam? The opposite sex is no mystery to me. They'd as soon box my ears as hold me in their arms and dance around the room." *Besides, being the oldest daughter and my father and mother needing my help, there was no time—or money—for dancing lessons.* "Promise me something?"

Lina stopped waltzing and tipped her head. "Anything."

"That we'll always be friends. That we'll stay in touch—no matter what. Moving away and leaving my family will be hard enough. I don't want to lose you, too. You're the only one I can confide in."

The bedroom door nearest the stairway opened, and Prudence stepped out. She drew up, surprised, then her eyes glittered and a deceptive smile played around her thin lips, making Heather take a tiny step back. Yes, she actually would heed Bertha's warning.

Chapter Two

"It's a deal," Hayden Klinkner said, grasping Stef Hannessy's large, outstretched hand and shaking it. A warmth born of family pride spread through Hayden's chest. Here was their chance to expand business into another town.

Hannessy, the owner of Pine Grove's Night Owl Mine, clutched Norman Klinkner's hand next. Laughter reverberated around the stuffy office, the small shack built a stone's throw away from the mine's entrance.

"I look forward to doing business with you two," Hannessy said, looking between them. "I know I can depend on you to deliver the lumber I need on schedule—without having to count every single board to make sure all is accounted for. The Night Owl is booming, and I don't have time to waste."

"You know we will, Hannessy," Hayden replied. "Six weeks is plenty of time to mill the wood at our place in Y Knot, then deliver the order to you here in Pine Grove. What're neighbors for anyway?"

The six-foot-four Swede snubbed out his cigar. "Good. That timetable is firm. No buffer." He pushed his chair back, walked over to the grimy window, and peered out at the work site. Hayden, along with his father, followed. "If you do a good job, deliver the lumber on time, who knows where this will lead with the other citizens here. I'm sure this transaction will be good for your mill."

A burly man pushing an iron cart emerged from the mine. The conveyance rolled easily on the smooth rails. Smudges of grime dirtied the man's face and his steps were labored. He stopped. Brushed the dirt from his hands and clothes. Got behind the ore cart once again and continued toward the pole barn, several hundred feet away.

"Why aren't you using Pine Grove's mill?" Norman's serious gaze searched Hannessy's face. "Lundgren's been around longer than we have and is only a few miles away."

Hannessy turned, his eyes hot. "It pains me actually to go elsewhere. Really does. I wholeheartedly believe in supporting fellow businessmen." He shook his head. "I just can't count on Abner anymore. Worse, I don't trust him."

Hayden could tell this was a sore topic for the man.

"We've been friends for over thirty years," the owner continued. "Migrated to Pine Grove on the same wagon train. Shameful he's turned into a liar and cheat. I refuse to do business with him, or his nasty-mouthed wife. Many of Pine Grove's citizens feel the same."

Hayden didn't know the owner of their competition personally, not the way his father did. He'd met the man a handful of times over the years.

"I haven't seen Abner in several years," Norman said. "What's going on?"

"Nothing good. He's had a few men running the mill for him, when he can find 'em. Mostly, he stays home and drinks. Is late with the orders, if they come at all. Then he ends up billing almost twice as much as he quoted."

"That's a shame."

His pa's contrite tone gave Hayden pause. He glanced over to his father, several inches shorter than himself, noticing the gray around his temple and lines at the corner of his eyes and mouth.

"I'd planned on stopping by to say hello."

"I wouldn't advise it," Hannessy said. "He's bitter. Always stewing for a fight. And now that you've just contracted the largest order I've ever placed, there'll be no reasoning with him—especially if he's drunk."

His father was torn. Hayden could tell by the coin he was flipping in his fingers, a habit they shared. "We wouldn't want to push him into something he'd regret later, Pa. We best be getting back. If we leave now, I'll still have several hours of daylight left to finish up the lumber for the Holcombs' henhouse and a few other small jobs."

"That may be so," Hannessy said, then went

to the door and took his black Stetson from one of the hooks. "But I'm hungry. And I'm sure the ride will be much more pleasant with vittles in your gut. Let's get a quick bite in town first. My treat."

Looking left and then right to be sure no one was watching, Ina Klinkner stepped into the telegraph office on Main Street. She nodded to skinny Mr. Tracy, no taller than her elbow, who sat at his desk reading a book. The man's brown hair was as scraggly as ever.

A whisper of angst soured her stomach. She thought about the post she'd sent two weeks prior, *before* Mrs. Seymour had surprised them all with her visit. Now that she knew the owner of the mail-order bride agency in St. Louis, and the woman had been a guest for dinner in her own home, her deception felt all the worse.

All Ina wanted was for her son, Hayden, to settle his wandering ways. Find a nice girl like Evie Holcomb, marry and have lots and lots of babies. Was that so much to ask? Why on earth was he so particular and resistant to her promptings? Yes, he was an only child, and yes, she'd coddled him a bit too much. She would have had oodles and oodles of children if she could, but the Lord knew, that wasn't the case. Now that Hayden was grown, if he would just find a nice girl and marry, a baby, *the babies,* would soon be in her arms.

"Morning, Ina," Mr. Tracy said. He dog-eared his page and snapped the book closed. "You have a telegram you want to send?"

"No."

"Oh?" He stood and came forward. "Is this a social call then?" He winked, making her pull back.

"Certainly not."

A chuckle escaped. "Well, I didn't think so."

He waited as Ina considered her plan of attack. Should she even bring this up?

"Ina, I'm at the good part of my book, so I'd appreciate you saying what's on your mind."

Nervously, she glanced around.

"The longer you stall, the more curious I get."

"I'm expecting a telegram, Mr. Tracy," she finally said. "From St. Louis. A private matter. I don't want you to send it out to the house. Instead, I'll check here daily."

Surely Mrs. Seymour would have a match for Hayden. Especially since she'd spent the whole evening with them. The matchmaker and Hayden had conversed throughout dinner and dessert. Would she think it strange Hayden never brought the subject up to her? Ina hoped she'd presume he wanted to keep the correspondence private.

Shame for meddling once again in her son's affairs brought a scalding heat to her face. This last escapade, actually sending for a bride, had her walking on eggshells. If things turned out for the best, she promised herself she'd never interfere in his life again.

Mr. Tracy clucked his cheek.

"It's not what you think. But, please. Be discreet. No one is to know."

"Don't you worry, Ina. I've been known as all sorts of things, but a gossip I am not. Your secret is safe with me."

Chapter Three

At the sound of enthusiastic voices, Heather hurried out of the dormitory bedroom, then descended a flight of stairs onto the second-story landing. She gazed down into the entry, trying to see what all the commotion was about.

Mrs. Seymour is back!

The matron stood in her travel cape and hat with the excited girls clustered around her, and her carpetbag next to her feet. She reached for the ribbons under her chin and untied them. A warm smile and eyes shining with amusement replaced her customary stern expression.

"Ladies, please," she said, laughter lacing her voice. "I need some space to hang up my coat."

"We're just so glad you're home." Bertha bounced up and down on her toes. "Feels like ages since you left. How was the trip? Did you find Evie? How is she?"

Juniper, smartly dressed in her black uniform and crisp white apron, promptly took Mrs. Seymour's travel cape from her hands and disappeared. Prudence stood back watching, her sour expression a contrast to everyone else's happiness.

As soon as the young maid returned from hanging Mrs. Seymour's cape, she opened the tall double doors leading into the parlor, and everyone rolled in like a wave.

Heather all but flew down the long staircase, being careful not to trip. She hastened toward the parlor, not wanting to miss a single word Mrs. Seymour had to say. Heather missed Evie. Had the matron found her? Had she met Evie's husband? Wonderment blossomed inside her at the thought of the unknown marital act and, unaccustomed to such contemplation, Heather shivered.

"Please get comfortable, young ladies," Mrs. Seymour said. The matron smiled at her as she entered and gestured to the empty wingback chair by the hearth. Heather sank into the horsehair cushion. Clasping her hands together, she leaned forward.

"It seems I'm not the only one making love matches!" Mrs. Seymour beamed. "I'm sure by now you've all heard that last week our president, Grover Cleveland, wed his fiancée, Frances Folsom. In my travels, everyone was abuzz with the news. He's the first president ever to wed during his term. Quite exciting, I must admit." She walked a half circle then stopped, glancing at Juniper by the hall doors. "Would you please ask Dona to make afternoon tea?"

Juniper nodded and hurried out of the room.

"As I was trying to say in the entry—I missed you all very much. It's nice to know I was missed, too. I can see your impatience for news about our Evie, so I won't delay a moment longer. Evelyn Davenport is now Mrs. Chance Holcomb. I have to say, I like Mr. Holcomb. Although I don't condone what Evelyn did, taking my mail and reading it, then running off in the wee hours of the morning without telling me, I do admire her spunk and determination. Not to mention her bravery."

"What does Mr. Holcomb look like?" Kathryn asked, tilting her head and patting her chestnut hair, which was curled and styled on the top of her head. Her wide smile made her two dimples appear. "Is he nice? Are they in love?"

Mrs. Seymour fairly glowed with happiness. Years melted from her face and she rested her folded hands upon her heart. For one moment, her gaze darted to the painting of her and the Colonel above the hearth. "Please remember, Kathryn, beauty is in the eye of the beholder— but with that said, I can say unequivocally that Mr. Holcomb is quite handsome, in a cowboy sort of way. He and Evelyn love each other very much. It was easy to see in each and every one of their actions. What impressed me most was the way he looked at her." She stopped and smiled. "I don't think I will ever forget it."

A sigh filled with longing rippled through the room.

Every girl had stars in her eyes—except

Heather, who dropped her gaze. If she had her choice, she'd stay right here in St. Louis with her family. Something must be wrong with her to think love was for romantics. If she had to marry—which she did—friendship, compatibility, and a hardworking man would suit her just fine.

"What's her home like?" Lina asked from the velvet settee.

"They live on a ranch a few miles out of town. The land is beautiful. There is a big barn and several outbuildings. Mr. Holcomb is a rancher and has a small herd of cattle. The home is newly constructed with a front porch, a rock fireplace, and a luxurious large cooking stove."

"But Evie can't cook!" Darcy said, her eyes going wide. "I remembered she told me that once. How is she getting on? Are they starving?"

Laughter erupted. Mrs. Seymour waited until it died away. "That may have been true when she left St. Louis, but she's been taking cooking lessons from a kind woman in town. I enjoyed a beautiful dinner she'd prepared for Mr. Holcomb's birthday."

"It's all so dreamy," Kathryn gushed. "I'm happy for her."

One of Mrs. Seymour's eyebrows arched and her smile disappeared. "Everything may have turned out beautifully for Evelyn, but don't any of you get fanciful ideas of your own. Evelyn was lucky—blessed, even. The results of her actions could have turned out quite differently. In choosing matches for you, I will make every effort to ensure my bride ends up with a law-abiding, God-fearing man."

"I wouldn't consider doing something so reckless," Prudence said. "Only a servant with no future would try something so irresponsible. With Mrs. Seymour's stamp of approval, the bachelors we marry will be pillars of their communities, as well as financially stable."

Prudence's smug expression galled Heather.

Juniper reappeared with a large silver server filled with blue-and-white china teacups and a handful of silver spoons. She carefully set the tray in the middle of the coffee table with a soft rattle from the stacked dishes. Napkins, two dainty creamers, and a sugar bowl rounded out the cluster of cups. The maid glanced over at Mrs. Seymour. "The tea will be ready shortly, ma'am."

Later that evening, while Heather reclined on her attic cot with her volume of *Jane Eyre*, Juniper hurried into the room. The dark-haired maid came straight to Heather's bedside and handed her a note.

"From the matron," she whispered, darting glances at Bertha and Lina.

Heather's stomach clenched. "The talk?"

Apprehension born of homesickness and dread swirled in her tummy, souring the warm milk she and the other girls had consumed with their bedtime snack. Her eyes darted to the delicate iron cross hanging above the doorway.

"I don't know, miss. She said for you to come straight away."

Heather sat up, placing her feet on the chilly floorboards as Juniper hurried off. Lina and Bertha sat up too.

Heather opened the folded note to find a single sentence.

Please come to my office right away.

She read the words silently. *My life will change tonight.* Refolding the communication, she placed the note on her pillow.

"A match?" Bertha whispered with enthusiasm.

"Can't be anything else," Lina added, clasping her hands together. "Her summoning you this late can only mean one thing. Heather's going west!"

The pointy hands of the clock sitting on the shelf above the washstand said the time was 7:10.

Bertha's genuine smile made her face shine. "Several letters have arrived while Mrs. Seymour was gone. Perhaps she's had a chance to read them through, make matches. Maybe there will be more."

Heather tried to ignore the dreamy expression stealing over both her friends' faces. She stood, straightened her skirt and shirtwaist, then glanced at her reflection in the mirror at the end of the room.

"Go on," Bertha encouraged. "She's waiting. And don't you dare stop to talk to anyone else when you're finished. Come straight back here and give us the good news."

Heather nodded, passed through the threshold, and closed the door softly. She took a slow step, thinking of Melba's birthday next month. Another step brought images of her Aunt Tillie's growing belly, and the baby coming soon. Her brother Travis had been courting his girl for a good year. An announcement was sure to arrive within months. So many events she'd miss—especially with the people she loved.

The trip from the third floor to Mrs. Seymour's office was the longest of her life. A million thoughts tumbled through her mind. When her foot hit the first floor landing, the idea of never seeing any of her six brothers or three sisters again brought a surge of hot tears to her eyes.

Heather paused in front of the office door. She mustn't let Mrs. Seymour know her true feelings. She had to do this! Her family couldn't support her any longer. Her mother was counting on her finding a husband, and believed she was eager to go west and marry. Resigned to her lot, Heather dashed her tears and forced a smile onto her face, praying her expression covered her breaking heart.

Chapter Four

Lifting her hand to knock on the office door, Heather was startled by its pronounced quiver. Resolved, she fisted her fingers and rapped on the pinewood door.

"Come in."

As expected, Mrs. Seymour was seated behind her desk. The spectacles she wore only while reading were perched on her straight nose. The window beside her desk stood open a few inches and the scent of roses from the backyard permeated the air. A stack of three or four opened envelopes sat to one side of the desk amid knickknacks and picture frames.

"Heather, please, make yourself comfortable." A twinkle played in the matron's eyes as she gestured to the chair opposite her.

"Thank you, ma'am." Heather made herself respond in a clear tone, although her insides were quaking. In a matter of minutes, her fate would be sealed. "Juniper said to come right away."

"I hope you didn't mind my summoning you so late."

Heather shook her head.

Mrs. Seymour's smile widened. She looked happier than Heather could remember.

The older woman swiveled back and forth in

her chair as she gazed at her. She made several small approving sounds in her throat, and then asked, "Would you care for a cup of tea? Dona is still up puttering around the kitchen. If you'd like, I can ask her to brew some."

The matron seemed to be assessing her. She'd do well to remember to keep her wits about her. Again, Heather shook her head. "No, thank you, ma'am. I'm fine."

Mrs. Seymour tented her fingers and leaned forward. "You look tense, Heather. Is everything all right?"

She swallowed. "Just fine."

The matron nodded. "Good. And things here in the house were uneventful in my absence?"

Heather shifted in her seat. Should she say something about Prudence and her habitual verbal attacks on Bertha and the others? Best not. If the matron gave Prudence a talking-to, things might get worse.

She nodded. "We got on just fine—but we're happy to have you back," she finished quickly. *That's the truth, pretty much.*

"I'm pleased to hear that. As much as I enjoyed the trip to Montana, and visiting with Evelyn and her new husband, I'm glad to be back home in St. Louis. The last two weeks reminded me of my early years with the Colonel, traveling around with the army, meeting people and seeing new places." Her eyes became misty.

She must have loved her husband very much.

"Now, I'm sure you have some suspicions why I called you into my office, so I won't keep you in suspense any longer."

Heather could feel it in her bones. Mrs. Seymour *thought* she was about to make her very happy.

"I believe I have a match for you, Heather. In addition, it's not just *any* match, but a *wonderful* one. A match of a lifetime!" Her enthusiasm practically bubbled over. "You see, the hopeful groom-to-be is from Y Knot, Montana, where I've just visited. And also where Evelyn lives. She assured me she likes the town and people ever so much and is happy there. I think you could be also." Mrs. Seymour waited for her reaction.

Evie?

Heather hadn't dreamed she might end up someplace where she knew someone. Especially a friend. A warm feeling took her by surprise. Hope welled up inside. She nodded.

"That would be nice," she heard herself saying.

"And not only that, but I've met the young man and his family. Had dinner in their home. I wouldn't even need to get a statement from the town minister."

"Oh," was all she could say.

"His name is Hayden Klinkner. He's twenty-eight years old." Mrs. Seymour picked up a sheet of paper from the top of the stack. "His family owns the lumber mill and they live on the outskirts of town. Mr. Klinkner has a small home that connects with his parents' home by a charming covered walkway."

She glanced up.

All Heather could think of was that she'd be in the same town with Evie. That in itself made this whole affair more palatable.

She took a steadying breath. "You've met him then—Hayden Klinkner?" She tried the strange name on her lips.

"Yes. He's quite a likable young man. And handsome! Read his letter and see if he might be someone you'd be interested in. The family is honorable. Of course, the decision is yours to make."

When Heather took the sheet of paper, it quivered in her hand.

Mrs. Seymour smiled. "Every young woman is nervous, Heather. It's nothing to be ashamed of."

"Why me?" Her voice sounded like her six-year-old cousin.

Mrs. Seymour stood and walked around her desk, then stopped at Heather's side. She cupped Heather's chin and looked down into her face. "I've been watching you closely. You have a kind heart. You're loyal and strong, and battle for your friends when others try to hurt them."

She knows about Pru!

"Also because I sense there are things you aren't telling me about yourself. Some deep wound I see in your eyes. I think a nurturing family is exactly what you need. Someone to chase away the shadows from your heart. Ina, Norman, and especially Hayden Klinkner, are the people to do just that."

Heather swallowed, still staring into Mrs. Seymour's eyes. The older woman dropped her hand and went over to the side table to look at a small photograph of the Colonel. "And because I want you to have some of the happiness I found in my marriage. I think you will." She turned back around to face her.

"Now, take a few minutes to read the letter while I make my rounds and say good night to the girls. We'll talk tomorrow about your decision. But, please, leave the letter here when you depart and don't share the details with any of the other girls just yet. If you turn this chance down, I'll have to try to match him with another, and young ladies don't fancy being second choice."

When Mrs. Seymour left, Heather brought the single page closer to the lantern.

Dear Prospective Bride,
Hello. My name is Hayden Klinkner, and I live in a small western town called Y Knot, located in Montana Territory. I

am twenty-eight years old and more than anything, I desire to wed, settle down, and start a family—right away. I have lived in this town for fifteen years, coming from Wisconsin with my mother and father. We are lumbermen by trade, and own the local lumber mill—which supports our family beautifully.

I am tall, have hair the color of corn silk, and blue eyes. I am a churchgoing man, and many persons of the opposite gender have told me I am handsome. The weather is simply beautiful here, prettier than I have ever seen it. If you choose to come, I believe you will love the funny sunflowers and delicate petunias around my mother's garden. I promise to take good care of you, and the children, if we are so blessed. My mother and father, the good people that they are, promise to help in every way to make our lives easier.

Heather paused, a bit confused. Hayden Klinkner was certainly different! Very attached to his parents, or so it seemed. His writings reminded her of the novel she was halfway through, more than a letter from a man. Her brothers would never write such curious things. But then, her brothers could shape steel into useful creations and household necessities. Reading and writing were not their strong points. Maybe he was a dandy more than he let on. She wouldn't like that. She recalled Mrs. Seymour's glorious report. Still, something inside felt a bit off, but she couldn't put her finger on it. She shushed her inner voice and kept reading.

> Please do not delay. Send a telegram to Y Knot in care of Klinkner Mill with your acceptance. After meeting Evie Davenport, I am more than eager to meet a bride of my own.
> With respectful admiration,
> Hayden Klinkner

Heather slowly reread the post, then folded the paper and placed the letter back on the large mahogany desk. *Hayden Klinkner. Mrs. Hayden Klinkner. Heather Klinkner.* She'd be living close to Evie. Having a friend in the same town would be so wonderful. Then again, traveling was a luxury, one her mother and family could not afford. Once she arrived out west, she was pretty sure she'd never see St. Louis again.

She took a deep breath and turned.

I have much to think about tonight.

The next morning, Heather was on pins and needles. Excited pins and needles. She rose early and dressed quietly, careful not to disturb Lina or

Darcy. They'd questioned her far into the night, grilling her with all sorts of questions she had to avoid. Promising to tell them everything the next day, they'd given up and gone to sleep.

Hayden Klinkner!

A jolt of pleasure zipped up her spine as she descended the stairs. Her conceived image of him had kept her awake most of the night. She was going to be married. And soon.

Heather knocked on the office door. When Mrs. Seymour called for her to enter, she ducked inside, finding it impossible to keep the smile off her face.

"You look happy, Heather."

"Yes, ma'am. I am."

"That's wonderful. Does that mean you're going to accept Mr. Klinkner's proposal?"

"Yes. I've decided to marry him."

Mrs. Seymour placed her hand over her heart. "Wonderful news. I think you and he will be happy together. May I ask you something?"

"Of course, ma'am."

"When you first came to the house, I felt you were unsure about being a bride. Was I correct in my assumption?"

Shocked, Heather glanced away. All along she'd thought she'd hidden her feelings so well. "Yes, ma'am. I was hesitant about being a bride. But now . . ."

"Yes?"

"Since reading Mr. Klinkner's letter, I just, well . . ." She felt her face heat.

"You don't have to explain a thing to me. I understand."

"Your personal recommendation helped a lot, too. That means so much to me."

"Well, good. Now we need to get that return telegram sent and your things packed. You'll want to say good-bye to your family, I'm sure. Also, respond with a letter of your own, telling Mr. Klinkner of your dreams and hopes. Remember, he can't read your mind. Now, while you're in this first bloom of your relationship, it's the perfect time to share everything in your heart. You'll see it's easy, and if you get into a habit of talking and sharing, your life will be as wonderful as the two of you make it."

Heather concentrated on what the matron said. She wanted that for herself and Hayden. A life of love.

"Now, off with you. Breakfast will soon be served."

Chapter Five

This is it. My destiny awaits. Keenly aware of her jittery insides, Heather glanced out the window of the Wells Fargo stage and took in the main street of her new home, thinking how small and primitive everything looked. They passed a telegraph office, reminding her of the telegram she'd sent accepting Hayden's proposal. People on the boardwalk stopped and stared as the stagecoach rolled by. The two boys who had traveled with her from Waterloo stuck their arms out the window, waving at friends.

Now that Heather had warmed up to the idea of marrying Hayden Klinkner, she was actually excited—giddy, in fact. She'd care for him, work alongside him if need be, *share his bed!*

Heat scorched her face at the last thought, and she breathed in deeply. Within moments, she'd be face-to-face with her future husband for the very first time.

As the transport creaked to a stop, Heather pinched each cheek several times, making her eyes water, then dabbed at her grit-covered forehead with a hanky. As best she could in the warm, cramped interior, she stood and smoothed the fabric of her jade serge skirt, then gathered her carpetbag from beneath the seat. She licked her lips.

Without waiting for the driver, the boys flung the door open and jumped out. Steeling her courage, Heather grasped the supple leather loop hanging next to the rickety stagecoach door and carefully stepped from the wiggling conveyance, down to the step, then to the ground, thankful for the sturdy feel of the packed earth as she set her boot to the street. With moist palms and a trip-hammer heart, she glanced around for Hayden.

Two wagons passed in front, then a buggy and three saddle horses. Cowboys, more than she'd expected, walked to and fro with jangling spurs. She looked down the boardwalk again, still not seeing anyone matching his description.

He said he'd be here.

A man approached, smiling broadly at the two boys, and gathered them into a hug. Feeling conspicuous and grimy, she stepped to the side as the stage driver came around and, with the help of a man he'd corralled, lowered her trunk to the street. The driver straightened up and dusted off his hands. He took a quick look at his pocket watch. "We're right on time. Would you like this delivered to the hotel, Miss Stanford?"

The fact that Hayden Klinkner might not show up to meet her never entered her mind. "Um, I'm not sure . . ." *My money won't go far paying for room and board for long.*

Her heart felt like a stone wedged between her ribs. "Just go ahead and leave them here for now. I'm sure—he'll be here soon." She couldn't bear to say his name aloud in case . . . he'd changed his mind. "I have a few things I need to pick up in the mercantile anyway." The store was right next to the Wells Fargo stage office, and with all the people around, she felt her things would be safe for a moment. She nodded toward the two-story bat-and-board building. "I'll be right back."

Heather slipped into the cool interior of the store, thankful for the opportunity to gather her wits. She stood back as an older gentleman pushed the keys on the cash register while a man—dressed like all the other cowboys with scuffed leather boots, leather chaps, a well-worn hat, and a gun strapped to his hip—waited.

"Here ya go, Luke. Tell Faith and the young'uns hello for me."

The clerk handed the man a small, paper-wrapped item, then grabbed a handful of sourballs from an open jar. "Matter of fact, give 'em these." After dropping the sweets into a sack, he handed that to the cowboy too.

"Will do, Mr. Simpson." His voice was deep. Soothing. "Tell Lichtenstein I appreciate him getting this in so quickly." He put the item in his breast pocket and held the bag of candy. "Roady, let's go."

Another man materialized from the back room.

He came forward just as the tall, dark-haired cowboy turned. The two spotted her at the same time.

She forced her I'm-totally-confident smile onto her face and walked forward, feeling anything but. "Excuse me," she said, turning to the clerk. Her mind went blank and she glanced around, mentally scrambling for an idea of what to say next. She glanced up. A sign on the wall gave her an idea. "Would you have a small tablet of paper? Something I can use to send a post?"

Her writing material was packed away in her trunk, next to her four dresses, and the dainty heirloom china teapot her mother had given her as a wedding gift and wrapped in the blue blanket she'd had since she was a girl.

Also packed away was a soft white nightgown made by her Aunt Tillie that she was saving for her wedding night; a canary-yellow throw pillow sewn by Sally, edged with white eyelet lace; three sets of thick wool socks knitted by Anita; and a horseshoe for good luck from Ben. Peter had made her a metal candleholder with a miniature door and cutouts that looked like stars—something he was doing to make extra money. Travis had given her a store-bought mother-of-pearl hand mirror, and Morgan, the matching hairbrush and hair receiver.

All thoughtful gifts. Curtis and Sam, both

shamefaced for having forgotten, gave her heartfelt hugs, and Melba, a beautiful handwritten poem wishing Heather and Hayden every happiness. At the bottom of her trunk were the novels she just couldn't bear to leave behind. *Oliver Twist* and *Great Expectations*, both penned by the great Charles Dickens, and her favorite book, *Wuthering Heights*, by Emily Brontë. She was halfway through *Jane Eyre*, and that novel she kept in her carpetbag to read while en route.

Both men touched the brims of their hats. She gave a courteous nod, but kept her attention on the clerk.

"I do, missy. On the shelf next to the straight pins."

Heather glanced at the shelves, confused. "I'm sorry, I—"

"Pins and paper are side by side. Both starting with a *P,* mind you. But I'm happy t' get that for ya. You just stay put." He shuffled away.

The first man headed for the door. "Miss," he said politely as he passed. The other followed. He nodded, then much to Heather's relief, they were gone.

Looking out the window, Heather checked on her trunk. She glanced up and down the street. Still no Hayden.

The clerk was back. "Here ya are. The envelope is a nickel extra. If you want to post it now, I can do that too, for six cents."

"Thank you. I do." What was she supposed to do? Panic was beginning to get the best of her. Was Hayden just late? She took a piece of paper from the stack and jotted a quick note to Lina, letting her know she'd arrived in one piece, and that her husband-to-be was nowhere in sight. She tried not to alarm her friend, but did make known the fact she may be back sooner than anticipated. Five minutes later, she addressed the envelope and paid for the stamp. Stepping outside, she went to her trunk and sat down on it, prepared to wait as long as necessary.

"Yoo-hoo," a female voice called out. "Miss Stanford, over here."

Heather turned. An older woman standing next to a polished, fringed-top two-seat surrey, waved at her with a white kerchief. The woman smiled warmly, then approached, reaching Heather in moments. Heather swallowed.

"Excuse me. You're Miss Stanford?" she asked.

He *didn't* come! Hurt edged her insides.

The woman wore a blue dress that buttoned up the front. Her golden hair, salted with gray, was pulled back in a neat bun, and a small white hat perched to the side of her head at a pronounced angle, like a little white mountain goat on a steep cliff. Her eyes darted around and she twisted the hanky in her palms, apparently even more nervous than Heather, who finally found her voice.

"Yes. I'm Heather Stanford."

"I thought as much. You fit your description perfectly." She gave a small, edgy laugh. "Besides, you're the only young woman with a traveling trunk."

Heather nodded. Disappointment that her intended hadn't shown up to meet her descended. Was this his mother? Mrs. Seymour had mentioned the woman with true affection.

Mrs. Klinkner, if this was indeed her, stepped forward and gave her a brief hug, then set her away to get a good look. She must have liked what she saw, for her smile broadened across her face, reaching all the way to her blue eyes. "Welcome to Y Knot," she said. "I'm Ina Klinkner, Hayden's mother. He apologizes for not meeting your stage himself, but there was a complication at the mill today, something to do with Norman's steam engine valves, or stoppers, or some such." She swung her hand a bit impatiently. "I never did learn all the names of the contraptions over there. He's very possessive of the engine and doesn't even let Hayden tinker with it. Anyway, my son hoped you wouldn't mind too terribly much if I fetched you home myself."

Before she had a chance to respond, a tall, rangy cowboy with a silver star pinned to his shirt reined his horse to a stop and dismounted. He took the hat from his head.

"Miss," he drawled slowly. A band of sweat had his hair stuck to his forehead. He took his palm and pushed the hair back. "My name is Jack Jones. I'm the deputy in Y Knot. Are you new to town?"

Ina snapped straight, as if the man were encroaching on her son's private territory. "Good day, Deputy," she said.

Heather almost smiled. "Why, yes I am. My name is Heather Stanford. I'm from St. Louis."

"I assume by your trunk you just arrived on today's stage."

"That's correct." Heather couldn't help but appreciate his friendly smile and warm eyes. *Hayden could have been here if he'd wanted. Could have greeted me with a warm smile of his own.* "It's a pleasure to meet you."

"Likewise."

Without being asked, he picked up her trunk and lifted it easily to his shoulder, then started for the surrey.

"You mustn't bother yourself, Deputy Jones." Mrs. Klinkner flapped her hands around and called after him. When he didn't stop, she let her arms fall to her sides. "Well, thank you."

Ignoring the older woman, Deputy Jones turned back to Heather once he had her trunk situated on the back seat of the carriage. "I'll ride out and help you unload these. Hayden and Norman might be off delivering some lumber somewhere.

As a matter of fact, I believe I saw them headed out of town."

"No, no. No, you didn't," Mrs. Klinkner sputtered. She looked back and forth between them, alarm written in her eyes, making Heather wonder at the woman's sanity. "That's not possible. I just left them both at the lumber mill not twenty minutes—"

The deputy, quite sure of himself, gave her a confident smile and then handed Heather up onto the upholstered seat. "It's no trouble at all, Ina, being it's just down the road." He gathered his reins and mounted. "Shall we?"

Chapter Six

Biting back a curse, Hayden stomped to the tool shed in search of a larger wrench, leaving his father standing beside the steam engine that ran the big saw, situated outside the large milling shed on a small plateau. His father's homemade contraption had started acting up, unusual for his unique but well-built, dependable machine. If they couldn't get the engine to build enough steam pressure, they'd have to revert back to the water wheel they'd retired a handful of years ago. If that happened, filling Hannessey's order on time would become impossible.

Taking the red bandanna from around his neck, he swabbed sweaty soot from his eyes, vowing to sit in the bathtub for an entire hour tonight. He grimaced at his own smoky aroma. When he leaned over, flecks of soot floated from his hair into the tool bin as he searched. Grumbling, he sorted through the collection of wrenches, hammers, and handsaws.

"Hurry up in there, Hayden!" his pa called. "Pressure is finally up and climbing. We may be able to salvage this if you find that large, two-sided wrench. The one—"

Kaboom!

The shack's walls rattled, the deafening sound

making Hayden flinch. Tools fell to the ground. For a split second, shock kept Hayden rooted to the spot. When he realized what had happened, he dashed out of the toolshed and ran toward the steam engine where he'd left his father. He was nowhere in sight.

"Pa!" Hayden searched wildly over the ground. The hatch door to the steam engine swung back and forth. White-hot steam hissed from every crack or fissure of the engine. "Pa! Pa! Where are you?"

An agonizing groan made Hayden turn. The blast had thrown his father a good fifteen feet to the base of a small stack of lumber by the milling shed. Hayden ran over and fell to his knees beside his pa's body. Gently, he lifted an eyelid on his father's pale face.

"Pa, can you hear me? What hurts?" His father's right leg jutted out at an awkward angle, most assuredly broken.

A horse and rider came galloping into the yard. "Norman! Hayden! Where are you?"

Glancing over his shoulder, Hayden saw Deputy Jones dismount and run toward the mill.

"Over here, Jack! Pa's hurt!"

As Jack ran toward him, he saw his mother's carriage careening down the road. With Jack now at his father's shoulders, he scooted over to his legs. "Ma! Hurry! We need more help."

Before his mother could reach them, a young

woman ran to his side. She quickly assessed the situation, then went around to his father's bad leg. "I'll take this side." In a billow of green material, she squatted and gingerly slipped her hand under his pa's knee, then put her other hand under his leg between his calf and ankle. Shocked speechless, all Hayden could do was look at her.

"On three," she said. "We'll lift together."

Hayden swallowed, then nodded. "One, two, *three*."

His pa gave an anguished cry and his head rolled back and forth, the pain overwhelming even in his semiconscious state. They moved slowly, carefully, trying not to jostle him. As they neared the house, his ma ran and opened the door.

In the house, they crossed the parlor and took him down the hall and into his parents' bedroom where his mother yanked the covers off the bed. They crowded onto the one side, then lowered him to the mattress.

Once he was down, the girl straightened out his good leg, and carefully repositioned the bad.

"I'm on my way for Dr. Handerhoosen," Jack called as he hurried out the door. "I'll be back as quick as I can."

Except for his father's ragged breathing, quiet filled the room. The young woman stood back, her eyes evaluating the situation. His mother looked as if she might faint.

"Ma, sit here," Hayden said, pulling her cherrywood rocker close to the side of the bed. He took her arm and helped her to sit.

"There must be something I should do while we wait for Dr. Handerhoosen," she said, her voice quaking.

The young woman came forward. "I'll get a cool rag for his head if you tell me where you keep your linen."

Thankful for help, Hayden said, "In the hall cabinet."

Who was she? He had no idea. His mother had been agitated for several days, and he'd wondered at the reason. She'd burnt their breakfast, overlooked the things she went to town for, and forgot about church last Sunday.

Something was amiss, but she'd denied it every time he or his pa had asked. Then she'd practically begged him to accompany her into town today. If not for the steam engine, he would have. Now this stranger, this girl—no, *woman*—showed up in his mother's surrey. Did she have something to do with his ma's strange behavior? The way the girl looked at him, regarding him intently with her pretty green eyes, he'd think she knew him.

Swishing back into the room, she stopped at the opposite side of the bed and unrolled a damp washcloth. She gently wiped away the grime from his father's face, then folded the cloth and placed it on his forehead. Taking the coverlet his mother had pulled off the bed a few minutes before, she gently covered him.

Feeling dazed, he couldn't withstand the suspense any longer. "Have we met?"

She stiffened. Glanced away. Her cheeks, which had been such a charming peach color before, all but turned white.

Hayden scratched his head. "Did I say something wrong?"

Her chest rose as she took a deep breath. "I'm Heather. Heather Stanford."

She acts as if the name Heather Stanford should mean something to me.

Her brow furrowed.

He felt the distinct impression he'd offended her in some unknown way.

"From St. Louis."

He shook his head. "I'm sorry. I don't recall our meeting. Are you a cousin to my mother, or something?"

Heather Stanford suddenly looked confused. Or upset. Why the heck should she be annoyed with me? I've done nothing to offend her.

With a wobbly smile, she reached out and placed a warm hand on his arm, her eyes searching his. "I'm so sorry to meet under these terrible circumstances."

Now he was *really* puzzled. He looked down at her fingers, their warmth and the feelings they evoked inside him perplexing him even more.

Clearing his throat, he struggled to get his thoughts together. "I'm so sorry, miss. The blast and my father's broken leg have befuddled my brain." *I didn't recall your name. Our meeting, or anything about you!*

"That's all right, and understandable with what's just happened."

Something in her tone made him think that wasn't quite true.

"I'm Heather, your mail-order bride."

Chapter Seven

Mail-order bride! Be hanged! He took a swift step back and her hand fell away. "I'm sorry, but that's not possible. Even as shocked as I am, I wouldn't have forgotten a bride—especially since I don't want one!"

When his mother stiffened and tried to turn away, everything became quite clear.

"Mother? Tell me you didn't send for this young, ah"—he cleared his throat—"lady." *Oh Lord, that's exactly what she's done.* For years she'd been obsessed with his settling down. Getting married. Starting a family. She'd finally taken matters into her own hands.

He dared another glance at Heather, this time acutely aware of his grubby clothes and soot-covered face. He must look a sight. Well, why should he care? She wasn't *really* his intended. As soon as she learned what his mother had done, no doubt she'd be on the next stage back to St. Louis.

Her icy gaze held his. Of medium height, the top of her head came even with his shoulder. She'd pinned her glossy black hair back in a bun. She was attractive, indeed. He'd be a liar to say otherwise.

• • •

Hayden Klinkner had never wanted her! Hadn't written the letter! Knew nothing about this! Unable to look at him a moment longer, she turned back to the window, trying to stop the shaking now consuming her body. *How could this happen? Why, Lord? Why now? No sooner had I embraced the idea of a husband, actually wanted one, and he's taken away. He never even knew I existed.* The unfairness and humiliation was enough to crush her soul.

One scalding drop slid down her cheek, which Heather quickly dashed away. She must pull herself together, fight the all-consuming desire to run from the room.

A sharp movement caught Heather's eye. "People! Coming down the road."

Hayden stepped over to the window, making her keenly aware of his male presence, his tall stature. When he leaned his forearm onto the sill to get a better look, the seams of his shirtsleeve strained from the strength of his arm.

Hayden nodded, casting an awkward glance in her direction. He didn't like the situation any better than she did.

"The townsfolk," he said. "They must have heard the explosion."

Several men carrying rifles led the way. The crowd parted hastily, and Jack Jones galloped through, closely followed by a beat-up old buggy that must be carrying the doctor.

"They're here," she said with relief, trying to think of anything except the man beside her. She kept her gaze safely trained far from him and on the crowd.

"Go home, everyone!" Jack's voice boomed through the glass. "Norman's homemade steam engine must've gotten too hot and blew. His leg is broke but Hayden and Ina are all right. The doc is here now to take care of Norman."

"You need anything?" one man asked.

The deputy shook his head. "Nope. Dr. Hander-hoosen is here."

Mumbling, and obviously concerned, the townsfolk turned and started back the way they'd come.

Heather breathed a deep sigh. Thank goodness the doctor was here. She glanced at Hayden's father, whose soft moans were almost imperceptible. His face was pasty white and his eyes were clenched shut, causing a multitude of creases to fan out from the corner of his eyes and line his forehead. Her gaze drifted over to the older woman looking so small in the rocking chair.

Heather felt horribly guilty that she could be upset with Mrs. Klinkner at such a time, but she couldn't stop her feelings. *How could Hayden's mother do such a thing? Did she think her son would just comply with his mother's wishes, marrying a stranger just because she wanted him to?*

Now the letter made perfect sense. *Corn-silk hair! The weather is simply beautiful, prettier than I've ever seen it! Funny sunflowers and delicate petunias!*

What man talks like that? None that she knew! Giving herself a mental shake, she put away her hurt in order to concentrate on the patient. What was done was done.

Heavy footsteps sounded on the porch, then the opening door brought her face-to-face with Jack Jones and an older man carrying a small black bag in one hand and two long flat boards in another. The doctor looked down at Norman and then up at her. "I'll need you to cut a sheet into long, wide strips. And boil up some hot water."

Heather nodded. She also needed to get Mrs. Klinkner out of here before they started to work. She took Ina by the arm and helped her stand. "Mrs. Klinkner, can you please show me which sheet I can use?"

"Yes—er, I mean, no." Ina looked befuddled. "I need to stay here. Help the doctor."

The men gathered around the tall four-poster bed, leaving Mrs. Klinkner up to her. "You'll help the doctor by showing me which sheet to use."

Mrs. Klinkner glanced back and forth until

Heather shepherded her toward the door. Heather ignored Hayden's thankful expression.

"Let me know if I can help in any other way," Heather said, then pulled the door closed. She propelled Ina down the hall until she saw the kitchen. "Here we are."

Mrs. Klinkner stopped as if just now remembering what was going on in the bedroom. "I need to go back and help Norman. He's hurt. Hurt bad. They'll need me to—"

"You just sit down here, Mrs. Klinkner," Heather insisted, directing her to the table and pulling out a chair, one beautifully handcrafted with intricate detail.

Heather took the kettle off the stove and stepped up to the pump at the sink. Just as she primed the pump, a piercing cry resounded through the house, making her drop the kettle into the dishpan with a noisy clatter. She turned, looking at the hall that led to the bedroom. *Poor man!*

Her second-oldest brother, Morgan, had broken his leg when his horse fell on him three years ago. He'd been lucky not to lose the use of his leg, but the recuperation had been long and painful. He'd been left with a limp, something any young, virile man would despise, and her brother was no exception. She didn't envy Mr. Klinkner at all.

She glanced at Mrs. Klinkner. The woman's wrinkled hands gripped the edge of the table.

"He's going to be all right, ma'am. This is the worst part."

Heather needed to get the woman talking. After stirring the coals in the stove and adding several pieces of firewood to the belly, she set the kettle on top.

"What's your husband's name, ma'am?"

Mrs. Klinkner turned. Looked her in the face. She blinked a few times before saying, "Norman."

Heather nodded.

"And you must call me Ina," she added, surprising Heather. "No daughter of mine should call me ma'am. You're Heather and I'm Ina. We'll be friends." Ina looked as if she were trying to smile, but her lips just wobbled.

Again, Heather nodded, wondering if that were still possible. Would Hayden change his mind after his father had been taken care of and he'd had a chance to warm up to the idea? She wouldn't, *couldn't* think about it now.

"I'm going to get that sheet for the doctor. Is there any particular one you'd like me to use?"

"Any one will do, my dear."

Heather hurried off, wishing Mrs. Klinkner . . . Ina wouldn't call her *my dear*. That endearment belonged to Grammy Hatcher. Her grandmother had called her *my dear* until her dying day—at eighty-nine—and the memory always brought a rush of tenderness into her heart whenever Heather thought about her.

Taking the linen from the hall closet, she hurried back to the kitchen. After checking to see if the water was boiling, she found some scissors and cut the sheet into four-inch strips. Finished, she bundled the fabric into her hands. "I'll be right back. You just stay put."

At the bedroom door, Heather stopped. *Should I knock?* She didn't want to interrupt what was happening inside. Slowly she turned the knob and pushed open the door. The deep timbre of Hayden's voice as he spoke quietly to the doctor registered in her mind.

As she entered, the doctor, leaning over the bed and the bare leg of Mr. Klinkner, looked up. The clear view of the bruised and twisted appendage sent unpleasant tingles up her spine. She darted a look at Hayden and found him watching her with unreadable eyes. She set the strips on the dresser and quickly left.

With that done, Heather sat next to Ina, willing her nerves to settle and wishing the kettle would hurry up and boil. She was sure the doctor would be needing hot water soon.

"Ina," she began, searching for something—*anything*—to talk about. This waiting was terrifying. "How is Evie? I haven't seen her since she left the bridal agency."

"Evie?" An expression of delight took over the

woman's face. "Yes. She's been a pure joy since I met her, the first day she arrived. I didn't know it at the time, but she'd just met Chance Holcomb a few hours before."

Sudden cries from the bedroom made both women blanch. *"Arrrg! Arrrg! No! No more!"*

Several agonizing moments crept by in silence.

"Stop! Hayden, make him stop! Please, oh God!"

Ina bolted to her feet.

Heather grabbed her hand to hold her back.

"No. You mustn't go in. Let the men do what they must," she murmured. "It's better for your husband. He's going to be okay. My brother went through this a few years ago, and he came out with only a limp. Mr. Klinkner will be fine, too."

"But Norman is *old*. He may not be able to take the shock. If infection sets in he could lose his leg—or worse."

Heather tried to smile. "Why, that tough old goat? I hardly think so. I'll bet he can take anything sent his way." It was true. He might be a smallish man, but Mr. Klinkner had felt wiry and strong when she'd helped carry him in.

"How did the two of you meet?" she asked, diverting Ina's attention.

Ina darted a look at the windows, as if remembering back to the time when she and Norman had courted. "I was eighteen. Come to town with my ma and pa. They thought for sure I'd be an old maid." Her voice drifted off.

"And?"

She smiled, bringing an answering smile to Heather's face. "Norman noticed me right off. Said my hair was what caught his attention. Reminded him of corn silk on the first crop of corn." She laughed. "His mother didn't cotton to me, though. She had her heart set on him marrying Martha Linsour. But hearts don't take direction once they make up their minds."

Heather wondered if Ina even understood the direction the conversation had gone.

Ina hiccupped. "But now he might die."

"You have to have faith," Heather said. "Faith that God will bring him through this. Ask and you shall receive." Faith alone had kept Heather going more times than she could count.

"I just don't know. I . . ." Ina turned her hands over and looked at her palms.

Heather bowed her head. "Lord, please help Mr. Klinkner. Ease his mind and heart. Ease his pain. Direct the doctor's hands and keep infection away. Thy will be done." When Heather lifted her head, Hayden stood in the doorway to the kitchen.

Chapter Eight

In spite of his soot-covered face, Hayden's sincere expression rocked her. Heather dragged her gaze away, feeling dazed, even bewildered. In that split second, something meaningful had passed between them, something she didn't understand or could begin to explain. An errant thought of kissing him, touching her lips to his, brought a sudden rush of heat to her face.

Flustered, she stood slowly. "Is the doctor finished?"

Hayden stepped into the room. "He's done setting Pa's leg and now wants to get him washed up. Is the water warm?"

"Yes, it should be," Heather said.

Ina stood and went to Hayden, taking his hands. "How did everything go, son? What does Dr. Handerhoosen think?"

"It's a bad break. But Doc says his leg will heal right with rest and nourishment." He glanced over at Heather, then back at his mother. "He has a concussion and several abrasions and bruises, but no other broken bones. Dr. Handerhoosen says he's lucky to be alive."

Heather went to the kettle and poured a small amount of hot water into a basin she'd found under the sink and prepared to hand it to Hayden, but Ina took the bowl instead. "Does the doctor need anything else?" Ina asked. "Soap?"

"No," Hayden said, letting his arms drop to his sides as he assessed his mother. "Doc brought what he needed in his bag." He glanced at Heather again and a warm, unknown feeling squeezed her chest.

Ina nodded, then carefully carried the basin toward the bedroom.

Heather, nervous about being alone with Hayden, took the heavy iron poker and stirred the coals in the stove, needing to keep her hands busy and her gaze directed anywhere but at him. His vivid blue eyes and wide shoulders had her jittery. His presence made all coherent thought dart from her mind like minnows scattered by a pebble. The blond hair his mother had so carefully described in "the letter" was now dingy with charcoal dust, but every now and then she caught a golden glint that snagged her curiosity. *Get hold of yourself, Heather! He's only a man. And one who means nothing to you—now that the truth is out.* Knowing she should feel relief at the thought that he didn't want to marry her, she felt puzzled by the reality that she didn't.

The stuffy kitchen air coiled around Hayden. He went to the window overlooking his ma's potted flowers and plots of herbs and vegetables. Pulling the pane open, he welcomed the breeze that flowed in, crisp and refreshing, cooling his heated skin. Felt like just moments ago he'd been drinking his morning coffee and bidding his mother good-bye, ready for a productive day. So much had happened since. He swallowed, thinking of the tall order they owed to Stef Hannessy and the Night Owl Mine. How could he get that accomplished without a working engine and his father's help?

He glanced again at the woman. And what am I supposed to do about her?

She was younger than he'd first thought during their introductions in the bedroom. She went about the kitchen trying to avoid drawing attention to herself, which was next to impossible given her graceful neck, which reminded him of the swans that had taken up residence on Fallen Leaf Lake. The interesting curve of her cheek and the set of her eyes gave her an impish look, reminding him of a wood pixie.

She poured water from the kettle into several cups, then set the tea infuser inside one.

"I'm sorry for any inconvenience my mother has caused you, Miss, ah . . ." Darn! He couldn't remember her name.

She swished the tea infuser around several times, then moved the round device to the second cup. "That's all right, Mr. Klinkner. I'm sure I'll survive."

"Her name is Miss Heather Stanford," Jack

Jones said as he stepped into the room, followed by Dr. Handerhoosen. Jack stopped, a look of admiration on his face as he regarded her.

Hayden had a bad feeling he knew exactly where this was going. He wasn't interested in her, but Jack Jones surely wasn't a good match for such a charming young lady.

"She's from St. Louis, Missouri," Jack continued. "Tell me, Miss Stanford, what brings you all the way to Y Knot, Montana? Are you family to the Klinkners?"

Heather moved the tea infuser to the third cup, then handed the first to the doctor. "For Mr. Klinkner, if he's able. I thought you'd want his brewed weak."

"Yes. Thank you, miss," Dr. Handerhoosen said, then turned and left for the bedroom.

If the situation weren't such a tragic mix-up, Hayden might have smiled at the look of consternation on Heather's face as she searched for some reason, other than the truth, with which to respond to Jack's question. He was interested in what she would come up with.

"Actually, I've just met Ina, and the rest of the Klinkner family. I, uh—"

Hayden straightened. "She's a guest in our house, Jack, and since she is, let's not question her to death her first day here."

Heather gave him a look that said she could speak for herself, thank you very much, then turned back to the deputy. "That's all right. I don't mind Mr. Jones's questions. I'm a good friend of Evie Holcomb. I'm here to visit her and Ina offered to pick me up."

She can think on her feet, too. Good girl! Hayden hid his smile. Her answer wasn't a lie. She was no longer a mail-order bride per se, so why mention it now and confuse the matter?

"That's right," Hayden said with a small grin. "I do remember my mother mentioning that."

"Evie Davenport Holcomb, the mail-order bride?"

Heather nodded, after which her chin tipped slightly up, defensively.

"The one and the same."

"Well, visiting her and Chance is going to be tough. They went over to Pine Grove for a few days. Didn't say why."

Heather picked up her teacup and took a dainty sip. Hayden would love to be inside that head of hers to see what she was cooking up next. She swallowed and replaced her cup on the counter.

"Evie must've forgotten to mention that to me."

Jack's smile was a little goofy.

"That's just fine, miss." He smacked his palms together with a pop, then rubbed them forcefully, as if it helped him think. "Perhaps I'll stop out sometime for a visit."

Hayden started for the parlor, grasping Jack's forearm on the way and bringing him along toward the front door that was on the other side of the room.

Jack looked over his shoulder at Heather as Hayden propelled him to the door.

"You be sure and do that." Hayden's voice was low and soothing. "Anytime. That is, after my pa is feeling better and is back on his feet. We'll need to keep the place quiet until then. So he can rest."

Hayden opened the door, then took Jack's hand, pumping it up and down. "Thank you kindly for all your help. We're indebted to you, Deputy."

When Jack Jones stepped out without another word, Hayden closed the door and went into the bedroom.

Sitting alone in the Klinkners' parlor, Heather listened to the quiet. Several hours had passed since her arrival. Her stomach growled with embarrassing loudness, and she was thankful she was alone. She wondered if she should offer to make dinner. Ina had insisted on sitting with Norman, even though the man was asleep. Hayden had taken himself off somewhere, and she presumed it was the place of his own that Mrs. Seymour had mentioned, behind the small garden in the back of the house, connected by the covered boardwalk.

Soon after Hayden had shown Jack Jones to the door, Dr. Handerhoosen had come from Mr.

Klinkner's room and given her several instructions about things to watch for, as Ina was still befuddled by the accident. He promised to return early the following morning.

 The house was still. So different from where she'd grown up. Back in St. Louis, the household rang constantly with conversation and laughter. In a family with ten children, someone was always around. Privacy was nonexistent. Her whole life she'd shared a room with her sisters, and although they'd been crowded, no one seemed to mind. The boys were all jammed into a large loft their father had built as the children kept coming.

 She closed her book, thankful she'd had the novel nestled in her travel bag, and noted the comfort of the chair she was sitting in. It faced an elegant Eastlake settee upholstered in rich blue velvet, which complemented the cool blue and lavender drapes adorning the parlor windows.

 What most caught Heather's eye, however, was the Chippendale desk. The lovely piece of furniture sat behind the settee on the far wall. Two large doors were open, displaying the desk's slots, drawers and compartments. Her brother would be green with envy! Although Morgan worked alongside her brothers in the smithy, his true love was cabinetry and furniture building.

 Everything in this house was beautiful. She wished her mother could see it.

After Hayden had left, she'd ventured up the stairs, looking for the guest room. Her trunk was still somewhere outside, in the back of the surrey, wherever that was. She wouldn't disturb anyone now. She could do without. Tomorrow, when the doctor came back, she'd solicit his help—that is, if she didn't see Hayden first.

Hayden. Her betrothed. Well, not anymore. She sighed, then shook her head. She should feel happy. She *did* feel happy! She was now free to do her will. The world was an open book, her future unwritten.

Would there be a job for her in Y Knot? Should she stay here? Going home to face a disappointed family held little appeal. Melba's face had been alight with excitement for the first time in a year when Heather had read Hayden's letter to the family.

Resigned to whatever path her life was about to take, she pulled out her writing paper and poured out her emotions to Lina, the only person who knew what was really going on.

Chapter Nine

Hayden walked toward the back door, his eyes gritty from lack of sleep. Neither the dew on his mother's flowers nor the crisp morning air eased away his troubles.

Poor Pa! The pain etched on his father's face last night was burned in his mind like a cattle brand. This would be a bad go for him. Norman wasn't young anymore. He had seen more than a few signs lately that his pa was slowing down. Once his pa felt better and wanted to get up, and start back to work, keeping him down would be Hayden's job. Caring for his pa while running the mill, filling Hannessey's order, and repairing the broken equipment wasn't going to be easy. At least Ralph and Jed Hicks had begun cutting and delivering logs. He could set *that* worry aside, at least.

A gangly cockerel crowed from the top of the hen house, happy to be alive. The sound shot through Hayden's sleep-deprived brain like a lance. He threw the young cock an angry glare. "Hush, you mindless featherbrain! I don't know why you haven't ended up as Sunday supper yet. Your time's coming."

At the back kitchen door he paused, wondering if the young woman—*Heather*—would be up yet.

It was still early, not yet half past five. City folk didn't cotton to country folk's early hours, or so he'd heard. Heaped on top of the concerns over his pa and workload was the awkward situation with Miss Stanford. Her plight had him restless all night—and he still didn't have a workable solution. He could pay her fare home, find her a husband—or marry her himself to satisfy his mother and get her off his back.

Nope, *that* wasn't going to happen. A woman who needed coddling and cooking lessons, like that Evie Davenport, was the last thing he needed. Sure, Evie was pretty, but he didn't have the time or volition Chance had. Holcomb must have the patience of Job, sending Evie for instruction from his ma.

Hayden knew he was feeling uncharitable due to the circumstances and his lack of sleep, but by his way of thinking, a woman taking on marriage should already know how to do all those things—and more. She should be able to sew, clean, cipher, as well as see to the children and her husband with solicitous care.

An outburst of clucking drew his attention. Hayden glanced to the fenced-in chicken yard and noticed the hens were out of their boxes and fighting over scratch scattered around on the ground. *Strange.* His ma didn't usually get to them until midmorning. He shrugged. Everything was off-kilter. When it rained around here, it poured. And there didn't seem to be a hint of clearing in sight.

Hayden stepped inside, expecting a cold, dark kitchen—and stopped. Heather, up and dressed, was moving efficiently about the room. The aroma of frying bacon and buttered toast made his mouth water, and the way her soft blue dress clung to her gentle curves made him force himself not to stare. He gave his head a small shake. Turning, Heather came to an abrupt stop when she saw him, spatula poised midair.

He darted a glance to the coffeepot on the stovetop, hoping desperately she'd made coffee. She lowered her arm.

"Just finished perking."

She'd read his mind. Better be careful in the future. Keep his thoughts on their best behavior.

"Breakfast will be ready shortly, too."

A quick sideways glance showed the table set for three. "Thank you . . . for stepping in for my mother. Taking care of things." *Us.* "You don't have to, you know. If you'd rather go to the hotel, I can take you into Y Knot later this morning."

He went to the table, took a cup from his usual place setting, and crossed the wooden floor to the stove. The heat of the fire had the room toasty warm.

"I know I don't have to, but I want to. Since your mother feels better staying by your father's side, taking care of the house is the least I can do."

Her voice reminded him of the small stream that ran by the mill. He jerked his eyes away from her face and fingered his collar for a moment, then filled his cup to the brim. When he raised the brew to his lips and tipped the cup, he noticed she didn't have any herself. Embarrassed, he gulped down a scalding swallow and clapped the cup back on the counter, pushing past the pain.

She gasped. "Be careful! It's hot!"

"I know—I just—heck, I don't know how that happened." He wiped several droplets off his chin with his palm. His lips lifted in a wry smile at how ridiculous he was being, unable to remember the last time a girl had made him nervous. "I'm sorry. Have you had a cup yet?"

She shook her head no.

"How impolite of me." He brushed his hand over his shirt to divest it of the coffee he'd rubbed from his face. "Well, would you like one?"

A small smile played around her lips.

He most certainly had seen a grin when he'd scalded himself. *I can play cat and mouse, too.*

When she nodded, he went back to the table for another cup, and took it to the stove. This was the closest he'd been to her. She smelled nice. Her velvety-soft-looking hair reached just past her shoulders in one straight layer. He tried not to look too long into her eyes, but that was proving problematic because the emerald shade, speckled with gray, reminded him of the first green sprouts of spring.

"Thank you for bringing my trunk up last night," she said. She poured some sweet cream from his mother's small blue-and-white porcelain pitcher into her coffee, then stirred it with a spoon. "I discovered it this morning in the hallway."

He shrugged. "You're welcome. By the time I remembered, you were in your bedroom with the light out. I didn't want to disturb you." *Fibber. You stood there for a whole minute wanting to do just that.* "Miss Stanford—Heather—I want to apologize for . . . everything that's happened. I don't know exactly what to say, except that I wish my mother hadn't caused you so much trouble. She's been at me for years to settle down. Get married, start a family." He shook his head. "For as long as I can remember, she's been counting the minutes until she has grandchildren."

She studied him intently enough to make his conscience prickle, even though he'd had no hand in the whole affair. He shrugged again and looked away. "The last thing I want is for you to feel embarrassed. It's not like you were jilted, or anything. I didn't know anything about you." *Ah, hell. I best shut my mouth before I dig myself in deeper.*

She took a small sip and set her cup on the counter, glancing at the frying bacon. "It's all right." With the spatula, she turned the sizzling strips over and gave each a little pat. "As you said, you're not responsible. I'm sure everything will work out for the best."

When he caught himself shrugging a third time, he almost groaned aloud. He wasn't a shrugger! Someone strange had taken over his body! He took another sip from his cup, this time more slowly. And a lot more carefully.

When she turned, he noticed a black speckled feather hanging on the back of her hair. He reached over and plucked the plume off. When he held it up in question, she smiled and opened the oven door to a rush of heat. His mother's large clay pot was inside.

"For supper. I hope you don't mind, but I thought everyone would enjoy a roast chicken, and then tomorrow I'll make chicken soup. It's a good remedy and fortifier for anything that ails you. Your pa needs all the fortifying he can get."

"You butchered a chicken?" He stared at her with his mouth agape.

She nodded.

"I mean, you plucked and *gutted* it?"

Her face clouded. "I didn't overstep my bounds, did I? When I went out to feed them, there were so many. I didn't think you'd mind if I chose a male—since there were more than enough roosters running around." She held his gaze.

When she didn't back down, he stepped away,

putting a good three feet between them. "No, I don't mind at all. I'm just amazed." *Impressed.* "You, a city girl and all. Why, you're full of surprises, aren't you, Heather Stanford?"

She busied herself turning the bacon strips over again and running a fork through the eggs to scramble them. "Being the oldest girl in a family of ten does require one to learn the ways of life quickly. There wasn't time for lollygagging." She took a handful of fabric from the side of her dress and pulled it around to show him a dollar-sized hole she'd pinned up. "Caught this in the fence in hot pursuit of the rooster. Now I have some mending to do."

Her smile was warm and engaging. An image of her dashing around the chicken yard, as he'd done many times throughout his life, made him laugh. "Guess you do."

She gave him a chastising look.

He stopped laughing. "Ah, has Ma been out yet this morning?"

"Yes, about twenty minutes ago. You need to get her to lie down today. She's worn thin and needs some rest. I think she sat in that rocker the entire night."

He nodded. "I can do that. I'll go check on them both right now."

"Wait." Heather poured two more cups of coffee and gave both a good dose of sweet cream. She placed them on a tray and added Hayden's cup. "Here, take this with you. I'm sure they could use something hot in their bellies. Let your mother know breakfast will be on the table in about five minutes, and I expect to see her there. I'll have a tray for your father ready as well."

Heather watched Hayden walk away and then collapsed against the counter to get her balance. Mercy, Hayden Klinkner was *handsome!* The most handsome man she'd ever laid eyes on. Bathed, shaved, and in clean clothes, he could stop a runaway team of horses. His eyes did strange and wonderful things to her insides. She glanced down at her quivering hands, clasping them together. She needed to get ahold of herself.
   Why hadn't Mrs. Seymour properly prepared her? The woman had met him, and knew exactly who she was sending her to. She felt like a fool. Coming from a family with six brothers, Heather was no stranger to women swooning right and left whenever her oh-so-charming brothers were around. Travis was over six feet three inches tall, wide of shoulder, and possessed a smile that could melt butter. Even when Morgan was a boy, girls and women alike became tongue-tied whenever they looked into his eyes. Ben's hair was like a magnet to any female's fingers. Peter was just plain incorrigible, and that seemed to be the trait that attracted girls like ants to sugar. Curtis and Sam . . . well, they were young, still

just boys, but they seemed to be following in their older brothers' boots.

But Hayden Klinkner!

She closed her eyes and counted to fifteen.

He was exactly the kind of husband Heather didn't want. Thank goodness the wedding was off. She'd not have a man who turned every female head, or was the subject of girlish fantasies night and day.

She needed a friend, someone to talk to. How she wished Evie were available. She would know about Hayden. When had Jack Jones said the newlyweds would be back? Tomorrow, or the next day? If Evie would have her, she'd take her things to the ranch and spend a few days while she decided what her next move should be.

The smell of smoke and the sound of crackling hot oil made Heather come around with a start. Quickly, she wrapped a dishtowel around the handle of the skillet, then pulled the pan of shriveled, burnt-to-a-crisp bacon from the top of the stove and hurried toward the back door.

No, a man like Hayden Klinkner was far too distracting! The proof was in the bacon. It was for the best that the marriage had been called off. The wedding *had* been called off, hadn't it? She realized no one had said a thing about the subject since her arrival.

Chapter Ten

The Hitching Post saloon was just coming alive as the sun set over the three-story Cattlemen's Hotel, the tallest building in Y Knot. Piano music jangled. Men streamed in and out. Horses nickered and a pig scampered down the boardwalk, crossing past the front door.

As Hayden entered, he passed a couple of dirt- and manure-covered cowboys in desperate need of a bath. His nose twitched and he looked away. Several other men sat at a card table in the corner, and Roady Guthrie stood by himself at the polished mahogany bar, deep in thought. Roady's black felt hat was pushed back, and his boot rested on the brass footrest. He worked a toothpick around in his mouth, a habit of his.

Sawdust slipped under Hayden's boots as he walked over to his friend.

Roady looked over.

"Guess you heard the news," Hayden said.

Roady's face grew grim. "Awful thing to happen to Norman. How's he doing?"

"It's a pretty bad break. He'll be laid up for a while." Hayden pushed away the memory of his father lying twisted and broken on the hard-packed earth.

Roady shook his head in disbelief. "I'll bet. How's your ma taking it?"

"She's worn herself out sitting by his side all night." He thought of Heather and her request that he get his mother to rest. He'd tried all day, but she'd been adamant. Tonight would be different. He'd pick her up and carry her to the other guest bedroom if he had to, and lock her in.

"Evenin', boys."

Hayden didn't have to turn around to know who'd joined them. Fancy Aubrey's sexy purr would stand out in any crowd. The unique sound had a note of caring along with a dash of devil-may-care. He'd never heard the like. The woman had the corner on warm and willing. He and Roady turned at the same time.

"Evenin', Fancy," they said in unison.

Fancy looked them up and down. "Glad you made it out tonight, Hayden. I felt the explosion all the way here. I guess all of Y Knot did. Lucky the two of you weren't killed."

Abe returned. The bartender looked at Hayden expectantly. His skinny frame always reminded Hayden of a scarecrow. He wore suspenders over his bright red shirt to keep his pants up.

"I'll take a beer."

The bartender set his cleaning rag down and reached for a mug. "Fancy? You want something to drink?"

"No, thanks. The night's still young." She batted her eyelashes a few times and meandered toward the card table. "Let me know if you boys get bored," she said, winking.

Roady shook his head. "That woman is trouble with a capital *T*. Nothing like Tilly, who used to work here. Fancy is—well, fancy. And she darn well knows it."

That she was. Hayden had met her the day she'd ridden the stage into town. He liked her directness and confidence. Not to mention her curvy body and saucy smile.

Hayden picked up his glass and drained it.

Roady's jaw dropped. "What was that for?"

"What?"

"You just got here. How you gonna hang around with your one-beer limit when you guzzle your glass dry the first minute you arrive? You usually nurse a drink like a day-old calf. Something under your skin?"

Sure there was. His father was hurt and laid up for weeks. The delivery to the Night Owl Mine was never far from his thoughts. Not to mention Heather—young, pretty, with eyes that reached to his soul. Standing in the kitchen with her this morning, he'd longed to pull her into his arms and kiss her soft-looking lips. Knowing she was totally off limits made him want her even more. He couldn't help but feel guilty about her quandary even though he'd not been the cause. But he wouldn't tell Roady that.

"I've got to get my steam engine up and running again. I don't have time to spare with the large order we contracted with the Night Owl hanging over our heads. I can't understand what made that machine malfunction. It's a mystery to me. But I can't help thinking Abner Lundgren sure had a lot to gain from us losing the contract."

Surprise registered on Roady's face. "Accidents aren't unheard of."

"No. But usually there's a reason. Pa is the one who built that contraption and keeps it up and running, and he's pretty diligent."

Abe approached. "You boys want another?"

"No thanks, Abe," Roady said, pushing off the bar. "I need to get back to the ranch."

Hayden shook his head, following. "Same here. I'm heading back to the mill."

Dr. Handerhoosen was just finishing up in the bedroom when there was a knock at the front door. Being the only one around to answer, Heather left her after-supper chores in the kitchen and hurried through the parlor. *Now who could that be at seven o'clock in the evening?* Practically everyone had heard what had happened, and a handful of the townswomen had stopped by throughout the day, dropping off dishes for suppers and every kind of dessert imaginable, making her job of caring for Ina and Norman that much easier. But this was after proper visiting hours. Drying her hands one more time on her apron, she pulled open the door.

Chapter Eleven

"Evie!" A rush of emotion cascaded through Heather. She gasped and rushed into her friend's arms. Evie smelled sweet, like a strawberry patch in summer. Evie's embrace soothed her as if she were a frightened child on her first trip away from home. And, indeed, Heather felt like one. Seeing the familiar face of a loving friend was what she'd needed for days. When they parted, Heather felt the void.

"Heather—when? How? I'm so surprised!" Evie crinkled her brow in the half-quizzical, half-curious expression Heather remembered from their time together at Mrs. Seymour's.

A tall man stood a few feet away.

He must be Chance Holcomb, Evie's husband.

Evie reached out and cupped Heather's cheek. "And I'm so pleased to see you." She let her hand fall away. "Jack Jones stopped us in Y Knot and told us what happened at the mill and about poor Mr. Klinkner. He also said you were here waiting for me. We came straight away."

Heather took Evie's arm and pulled her inside. Mr. Holcomb followed, closing the door behind him.

Heather gripped her friend's hands in her own. "It's a long story, Evie, and I'll tell you the whole thing. But first, let me say how glad I am that you're back. I'd wanted to surprise you, but the surprise was on me when I arrived and you weren't here . . ." Heather's voice faltered and she dropped her gaze to a lengthy crack in the floorboard. "Things didn't quite pan out as expected."

She glanced up at Mr. Holcomb, taking in his face, the crease of worry between his eyes.

Evie smiled. "I've forgotten my manners again. I'll need to revisit my book of etiquette." When she looked up at her husband, he gave her a wink. "Heather, this is my wonderful husband, Chance Holcomb. Chance, this is my dear friend, Heather Stanford. We met at the mail-order bride agency in St. Louis. She was there when I left to marry you." She took hold of his elbow and hugged it tight to her side. "Chance is my knight in shining armor."

Mrs. Seymour had not exaggerated, Heather thought. The love fairly crackled between them.

"I'm pleased to meet you, Mr. Holcomb. Mrs. Seymour had many wonderful things to say about you when she returned from her visit here in Y Knot."

His face actually turned red, then a boyishly charming smile appeared. "I'm pleased to meet you, Miss Stanford. But just call me Chance. No need for formalities."

"I'll call you Chance if you call me Heather."

Evie started, then covered her mouth behind her hand and her eyes grew wide. "Oh my goodness! Heather, has Mrs. Seymour made another match?"

Chance's eyes opened wide and he began slowly backing away. "I think you two girls need some time to catch up." Setting his hat on his head and tugging it secure, he reached for the doorknob. "I'll just go into town for a while and see who's around."

Evie beamed. "Thank you for being so considerate." When he opened the door, Evie called, "Say hello to Fancy for me."

With Chance gone, the girls went into the parlor and faced each other on the sofa. "Can I get you a cup—"

"No, thank you," Evie said quickly. "I'm just fine. Where's Ina?"

"In the bedroom with Mr. Klinkner and Dr. Handerhoosen. They should be finished soon. Ina needs some rest. Please try to talk some sense into her."

"I will. But now, tell me how you came to be here in Y Knot, staying with the Klinkners. You look tired and worried." She reached out and touched Heather's hand. "As you can imagine, my mind is whirling like a windmill on a blustery day."

For the next fifteen minutes, the whole story poured out. Heather dabbed at the corner of her eyes with the hanky Evie had provided from her reticule. "Actually, I don't know why I'm crying," Heather said. "I'm relieved the wedding is off. But the whole thing is so embarrassing. Even though I know I shouldn't be, I'm ashamed."

"Don't you dare say that! You had nothing to do with it. Any man would count himself blessed to have you for his wife. Heather, you believe me, don't you? If anything, you have every right to be angry. But I'm glad to hear you're not holding the situation against Ina or Hayden."

"I'm not. I just know the last thing in the world I want is to be shackled to somebody who doesn't want me." When her voice wobbled on the last word, she took a moment to compose herself. "Who doesn't love me. I never really wanted to marry in the first place. This mix-up has turned into a blessing in disguise."

Evie clucked her tongue softly. "I can't believe Ina did that, but on the other hand, I should've seen it coming. She asked me many questions about being a mail-order bride. Also about Mrs. Seymour and the agency. She must have sent the letter before Mrs. Seymour came to Y Knot. I'm sure she feels horrible. And sending for a bride for Hayden, no less. Why, he's such a ladies' man. He's always . . ."

Evie snapped her mouth closed.

Heather stopped dabbing her eye and watched Evie closely, wondering what she'd been about to say. What did she mean, he was such a ladies' man? Was there something more? With brothers like Travis and Morgan, that something wasn't hard to imagine. Yes, Hayden was devilishly handsome, but other than giving her goose bumps and making her heart flutter wildly, all he'd been was solicitous toward her, and respectful and caring with his parents.

Evie's eyes brightened. "Have I told you about Trudy?" Evie asked, seeming to have picked up on Heather's silence and acting as if she hadn't been about to spill some important secret. "We write to each other all the time. She's married to a wonderful man, a farmer. They have plans to add on to their home as soon as—"

"Evie?" She wasn't going to let her friend change the subject. "Hayden's always what? What were you about to say?"

Evie flounced back on the sofa, then smoothed her skirt. "Well," she began, tipping her head to the side. "I've heard he likes to chat with the women—*all* the women."

"Chat? Is that all? Do you really mean flirt?"

Evie shrugged. "Well, yes. I suppose I do. Chance shared with me how angry Luke McCutcheon was with him when he took a liking to his wife a few years ago."

"Was he flirtatious with you, Evie? Did he make any unwanted advances? Maybe he's changed his ways . . ." Why on earth did she feel the need to defend Hayden Klinkner? She'd only known the man for a day and a half, for goodness' sake! He surely didn't figure in her future. *Not now, anyway. He could be the biggest ladies' man on the face of the earth, and it shouldn't bother me in the least.*

Evie looked to the hallway, obviously uncomfortable with the conversation. "Actually, now that I think on it, no, not any more than other men I've met here. He tipped his hat to me when I got off the stage, said hello a few times." She stopped. Glanced down at her hands in her lap.

"And?" Heather coaxed.

"Heather, Hayden's actions with others is neither here nor there. He's a fine man, I'm sure. I admire him very much. If you're attracted to him, I'd say you should tell him." Evie's eyes twinkled, reminding Heather of her sister Sally. "Before he knew Chance and I had married, he did give me 'the look.' "

Heather laughed, knowing exactly what Evie meant. "I've had 'the look' too, but only when he didn't think I saw him."

The front door opened and Hayden stepped in. When he saw her and Evie, he drew up short. He removed his hat. Heather thought she saw a moment's hesitation in his eyes before he proceeded forward.

"Evenin', ladies," he said, and stopped. Faint lines that fanned from the corners of his eyes attested to his fatigue. Whiskers the color of straw covered his jaw, which was set in a hard line. He looked as if he hadn't gotten a bit of rest since this morning. Even then, he'd looked exhausted.

"Evening, Hayden," Evie replied.

Heather couldn't miss the rosy color darkening her friend's face. It wouldn't be hard for Hayden to guess what—or *who*—they'd been talking about.

Evie leaned forward. "Did you see Chance on your way here?"

One corner of his mouth twisted up. "No. I came the back way cross-country. Was he in the wagon?"

"Yes."

"That explains it." He glanced at Heather, making her breath catch. Then he gave a conspiratorial wink. "Don't let me interrupt. I'm just on my way in to check on Pa."

They both watched him turn and walk down the hallway to the bedroom. The door opened and closed before either woman felt safe to say a word.

"Did you see it?" Evie whispered, leaning close.

"See what?"

"The way he looked at you. Respectfully, with a certain . . . I don't know. Glimmer. I couldn't put my finger on it, but I'd say he's been thinking about you, Heather. Has taken a liking to you. By all means, I'm no expert on Hayden Klinkner, but I've never seen him act or look like that."

Why does Evie's comment make me happy? Heather didn't know why, but it did. She'd wanted to go to him, ease the coat from his shoulders, and work the stress from his back and arms. She gave herself a mental shake, then glanced at Evie to find her friend staring.

"You saw it too! Didn't you! Your face looks like the pink roses around the carp pond behind the house in St. Louis. You can't fool me."

Evie's silvery laugh lightened the mood in the room. She stood and grabbed both of Heather's hands, pulling her to her feet. "Come on, I feel like that cup of tea now, before Chance returns. We have some planning to do."

The determined glint in Evie's eyes was something new to Heather. What was her friend up to? "Now, wait just a moment," Heather muttered as Evie dragged her into the kitchen and set her on a stool with a look that brooked no argument.

"You just sit right there, Heather. I know this kitchen like the back of my hand. As a matter of fact, I'm the one who brought over this wonderful strawberry tea. After we have a cup, I'll tell you what's perking in my little head—oh, yes, indeed!"

Chapter Twelve

Hayden donned his work shirt and sturdy canvas pants, then pulled on his leather boots. Three days had flown by. With the problem at the mill, despair was never far from his mind. He needed to get back to work—address the complications that had been robbing him of sleep, and get the timber for the Night Owl Mine order cut and into the milling shed. Before that, however, he needed to fix the steam engine or he wouldn't have a way to cut the wood once they had it. With June Pittman out of town, there wasn't a blacksmith to help repair the machine.

Hayden opened the door to his small house, went out and closed it, starting for the mill. He'd check things over there before going to his parents' for breakfast—and to see Heather. His pa was on the mend, thank goodness. The pain in his leg had subsided somewhat and he was sitting up in bed and reading the paper. At least one thing was finally headed in the right direction.

To his mother's delight, Heather Stanford was still here. The two women were inseparable, always laughing over the strangest things. The atmosphere in the house had gone from comfortable to downright pleasant. Moments he looked forward to all too much.

Today, though, Heather was moving into town, where she planned to work for Dr. Handerhoosen in the mornings, do Mr. Lichtenstein's books next, and help Berta May in her sewing shop later in the afternoons. Seemed the young woman from St. Louis was not only capable in the kitchen and with her needle, but also ciphered well enough to have kept the books for her family's blacksmith shop since she was thirteen.

Old Mr. Lichtenstein, with his German sensibilities, had taken a shine to her practical and forthright way the moment he'd laid eyes on her. The proprietor's mouth had gaped when she'd helped Mr. Simpson with a difficult addition problem he was having. A customer was returning two pairs of shoes that had been on sale, then added a slate, chalk, and several more household items. When Heather was finished, the figuring came out to the penny. A man looking for a wife—one that pulled more than her own weight—couldn't do better than Heather. It was almost too bad he *wasn't* looking for a wife. For a moment, he wished she'd descended on Y Knot five years in the future, when he would be ready to settle down.

Hayden smiled. Would he miss her? Sure, he would. All kidding aside, he'd grown used to clever conversation at breakfast, as well as the new recipes she'd shared with his mother. Yeah, he was going to miss her smile, the curve of her face, the way her eyes danced when he teased her. Sure, he was going to miss her—a lot.

On the road between the mill and the house, he stopped to watch as the new day topped the far mountain range. Golden beams of light shot through the clouds, turning them pink. This sight always brought a sense of awe.

"Hayden!"

He turned to find Francis, the young cowpoke who worked out at the McCutcheons' ranch, waiting by his horse's side, reins in hand.

Hayden hastened over to the boy. "Francis."

"Roady sent me. We need an order of lumber for a new barn for Luke's homestead. He wants to bring a handful of yearlings up from the main house and needs a place to keep them. Wondered if you might already have some milled, or if not, when you might."

Hayden gripped the back of his neck in frustration, craning his neck to the side, almost enjoying the resulting pain. The stack of lumber they'd built up over the month had disappeared, board by board, over the last week. He had a small stack for Holcomb's henhouse, but that was milled and spoken for before the accident. He couldn't in good conscience take on another order until he knew exactly when the mill would be up and running. Even then, not until after he'd fulfilled the obligations they'd already taken on. "I'm sure you heard what happened last week."

Francis's eyes widened with concern. "Sure did. Awful. Glad to hear your pa's doin' better."

"Thanks. Our steam engine is still broke, though. I can't give a date for the lumber until I get it fixed. I don't have what you need on hand, either. Luke in a rush?"

"Don't know," Francis answered. "I think he wants to have the barn up this summer, definitely before fall."

"I'm sure that's doable. Tell him I'll send word when I know a little more in a few days."

Francis nodded and mounted up, his horse pulling for rein. The stocky bay took a few impatient steps before Francis quieted him. "Will do."

Across the way, Heather stepped through the front door, a dishtowel in her hands. Hayden didn't even try to stop the wide smile that spread across his face. He watched as she sought him out, and his smile faded. Soon she'd be gone, and life would get back to normal. Normal *without* Heather.

She raised her hand and waved. "Hayden, breakfast is ready anytime you are. It's in the warmer, so don't worry if you're busy. No rush at all."

Francis sat a little straighter in the saddle—and why not? On the doorstep, with her hair up and wearing an ironed white apron, Heather was a sight. A creeping blush came up the boy's neck and blossomed on his cheeks.

"Thank you," Hayden called back. He ventured another look up at Francis as the boy still hadn't ridden away.

"Mrs. Holcomb's friend from St. Louis?" Francis asked without taking his gaze off her.

"That's right," Hayden said, feeling more than a little possessive. He waved. "I'll be right in." At her smile of acknowledgment, a bubble of sadness wedged somewhere in the region of his heart.

She disappeared back inside.

Keeping a secret in a town the size of Y Knot was next to impossible. Word of Heather's arrival had spread and the whole town knew about her—not all the details concerning his ma, and how she'd written the letter—but the fact that a beautiful young woman new to town was staying out at the mill. They knew she was a mail-order bride without a husband. Knew she'd soon be living and working in town.

And they know I have no claim on her.

Hayden breathed a small sigh.

"She's sure pretty, all right. Jack Jones is going all around town bragging he'd seen her first and is gonna marry her. All the men are asking all kinds of questions. In my way of thinking, she's fair game to anyone, as long as she'll have him."

Francis turned his horse to leave and glanced back. "Almost forgot." He leaned over and unbuckled his saddlebag, then rifled through the contents and handed a letter to Hayden. "When I picked up the mail for the McCutcheons, Mr. Simpson asked me to bring this out to you, seein' as how I was coming this way."

Hayden looked at the post, expecting to see Stef Hannessy's Pine Grove return address. Instead, it was addressed to Heather Stanford. "It's for Heather."

Amusement flickered in Francis's eyes. "Well, ain't she inside?"

"Of course."

Francis politely cleared his throat as if the situation were perfectly obvious to him. "Will you give it to her?"

"Sure—ah, of course." Hayden studied the cursive writing. "I expect you're right about her getting a lot of attention, Francis," Hayden added quickly, trying to divert attention away from his loss of composure. "We'll see how this all plays out." *Jack Jones?* He wasn't surprised after the show the deputy had put on the first day he'd met Heather. *He's not fit to wipe her boots.*

Heather hurried inside and glanced at the table to make sure everything was perfect. *My last breakfast with Hayden.* An underlying current of sadness tugged at her, but she tried to ignore it. Instead, she gazed at the pretty yellow and pink roses in the center of the tablecloth. They made her think of Mrs. Seymour and the girls in St. Louis . . . and her baby sister Melba, with her deteriorating health. Was she any better? Any worse? She'd sent a letter home asking, but hadn't told them of her own plight. Lina was the only one who knew about that.

"Everything looks lovely, my dear."

Heather turned at Ina's now familiar and cherished voice.

Hayden's mother stood in the kitchen doorway. Color had returned to her face. Now that Norman felt better, the older woman had taken Heather under her motherly wing, providing support that was warm and engaging. Hayden's father, grumpy this morning for being "coddled to death," insisted the pain was gone. He wanted to get back to work and snapped at everyone for their united front in keeping that from happening.

"Is Hayden on his way in?" Ina asked, opening the stove door and peeking inside.

"Yes. I hope you don't mind, but I've made enough for Dr. Handerhoosen too, for when he stops by this morning." *I've also packed my trunk and am ready to go.* The kind doctor was transporting her things to the boardinghouse. Hayden had offered but she knew the pressure he was under trying to get the order done at the mill.

Ina chuckled. "That's a fine idea. He's been coming out every morning and evening, checking on Norman. It's the least we can do." Her face clouded, as if she were sad this morning too. "The aroma of bacon drew me out of the room—that and Norman's grumbling for his breakfast. I swear, you don't really know someone until they're confined to a bed. I've never seen him scowl a day in his life. Until now. Later today, he's allowed to sit in the parlor as long as he doesn't put any weight on the leg or stay up for too long."

The strain around Ina's eyes was gone, replaced with determination and hope.

Heather turned and headed for the parlor. "Ina, that's wonderful news. I'll get his chair ready for—"

"You just stay put, young lady. I can take care of that myself. You've done more for us than a hundred others combined. I'm indebted." Her smiled wobbled and she glanced away. "It won't be the same around here without you."

A throbbing lump wedged in Heather's throat. *It won't be the same for me, either.*

Chapter Thirteen

When Hayden took the last sip of his coffee, Heather promptly rose and went for the coffeepot on the stove. He rubbed his belly, thinking maybe her leaving was a good thing, given his expanding middle. That had been one of the finest meals he'd ever had. Not only were the biscuits light and fluffy—and the bacon perfectly crisped—but she'd served mashed potatoes and gravy, with a thick slice of beef complementing two fried eggs. He pushed his chair back and made room to relax.

He stopped her at a quarter cup. "Thank you."

"My pleasure." Heather filled his mother's. She replaced the coffeepot and took her seat. Pushing her potatoes around with her fork, she looked disinterested in her food.

Ina smiled. "Heather said we had a visitor already this morning."

"Yes. Francis. From the McCutcheon ranch. He was looking for some milled lumber, enough to start a barn, but we don't have even a board left. I need to get our saws up and running, and soon can't come fast enough."

Heather took a sip of her coffee, gazing at him over the rim. Setting her cup in its saucer, she wiped her mouth with her blue-checked napkin. "Do you have any idea when that could be?"

"No. And that's what's so maddening. I have the Hicks brothers bringing in logs the rest of this week, but since June left to visit her mother, no one else in town has the ability or finesse to copy the parts of Pa's homemade steam engine. I've tried three times already, using her equipment, and failed every time."

"June is the blacksmith?" Heather asked.

"Yes, and livery owner."

"When's she coming back?"

"I'm not sure. The mill has never been shut down before. This accident couldn't have come at a worse time."

Ina reached over and patted his hand. "You'll work everything out, son. I have confidence in you."

Hayden had tried to keep the worry from his family. But now that time was short and they were in danger of losing the contract, as well as other orders, it was time everyone understood what was at stake. "If we don't find a solution, we'll have to forfeit the Night Owl contract by the end of next week." Frustrated, he drained his cup, then took his napkin from his lap and wiped his mouth.

"I'm sorry, Hayden," Ina said softly. "I didn't know."

"Speaking of Francis, that reminds me—he brought something for you," Hayden said, looking at Heather. His half-truth brought a rush of heat to his face. He hadn't forgotten. The darn post was practically scorching a hole in his pocket. Why the letter should interest him was a mystery. He should have handed it over the moment he walked through the door. He pulled it out and handed it to Heather.

"Go on and read it, my dear," Ina said. "I'll finish up here."

A knock sounded, then the door opened. "Hello in there." Dr. Handerhoosen came to the kitchen doorway and stopped. "I heard you all talking. I hope you don't mind my letting myself in."

"Of course not," Ina replied.

"How's our patient today?"

"Better. Eating his eggs and bacon," Hayden said.

The doctor nodded. "I'll check on him and be back in a moment."

"I've made you some breakfast too, Doctor," Heather said, backing toward the hallway. It was evident she was dying to read that letter. "I hope you brought your appetite."

He laughed, his eyes dancing with merriment. "As a matter of fact, I did." He rubbed his round stomach. "Bless you. I left this morning without a bite to eat." His smile covered his face. "Are your things packed for the ride back into town? I told Drit and Lou you'd be checking in at the boardinghouse sometime around ten."

When Heather darted a look in Hayden's

direction, their eyes met and held, then her gaze dropped to his lips.

Surprised, he picked up his cup, intent on draining it, before remembering it was already empty.

"They are, Doctor," she said and looked away, but not before her eyes softened with pleasure. "I'll be ready when you are. All I have left to do is tidy up the kitchen."

"You'll do no such thing!" His mother's tone was tinged with sadness. She'd never been happier than during these days with Heather, even with his father's accident. "You've been doing more than your share for days now. I don't know how we would've gotten through this ordeal without you."

"If you're sure."

Ina pointed to the stairway. "Go on now and read your letter."

Heather practically raced up the stairs. She closed the door and flounced onto her bed, staring at Lina's beautiful handwriting that brought a rush of happiness.

Opening the envelope, Heather had to dash away a wistful tear in order to read its contents.

> Dear Heather,
> Not be alarmed! How can you write me not to feel alarmed? I hope I receive

a second letter on the heels of this one telling me all is well, and you are pleased with Hayden Klinkner as your choice of husband. If I have to wait days to know what happened to you, I will travel to Y Knot myself to scold you in person—in Italian, no less! You have not lived until you have been on the receiving end of an Italian tirade! I will go to church today and light a candle for your safety and matrimonial bliss.

Heather paused, holding back a smile. She'd seen her friend in a passionate rant to a grumpy storeowner who'd been rude to Lina's sister. No, she didn't want to be at the receiving end of one of those.

As for me . . . As I promised my mama, I have delayed leaving for a few days and have been visiting my family every day. Now that I know I will not be staying in St. Louis, the warmth and chaos of my family has become dear to me—something to be savored, for I do not know when I will be enveloped by their love again. However, after my visits, I am also glad to return to the peace and quiet of the agency, although I miss you, my dear friend. The house seems empty without

Trudy, Evie, Megan, and you. That dreadful Prudence tries to lord it over everyone. She is worse since you have been gone. You were so good at putting her in her place!

Prudence torments poor Bertha dreadfully. I almost dumped the soup pot over that nasty woman's head today. I feel sorry for whichever man ends up with her! Darcy, Kathryn, and I band together to protect Bertha and the new maid, Juniper. But we cannot know what goes on behind our backs.

I am spending a lot of time in the kitchen. At least the other brides are becoming good Italian cooks. Too bad I won't be here to teach them how to make pasta noodles. Two days is not long enough.

I am looking forward to seeing Trudy again. I am also looking forward to and dreading meeting Jonah Barrett. What if I cannot make him happy? What if his son takes a violent dislike to me?

If you have not quickly written another letter, send me a telegram to let me know you are all right. I am off to church now to light that candle!

Your friend,
Lina Napolitano

After scanning the letter quickly, Heather took a few more minutes to reread the correspondence more slowly. She savored the words, even the parts about Prudence. Oh, how her homesickness doubled thinking of everyone at home, the agency, her sweet, dear little sister. The second time through brought a new wave of longing. And questions about her future.

Being a mail-order bride had gotten her to Y Knot, but Heather reminded herself that she had new plans now. She couldn't do what Evie had wanted; go after Hayden, pretending she wasn't interested until he took the bait. That just didn't feel right.

Leaving and venturing out on her own was the correct thing to do. Besides, she didn't have any other choice. Hayden hadn't changed his mind. He hadn't asked for her hand. Had she really expected him to do that? At the boardinghouse, she'd bartered to do some light cooking in exchange for a reduced rate of board. The proprietors, Drit and his wife, Lou, were delighted to take her up on her offer. The two-story house across from the sheriff's office was often filled to capacity, and they were tired of the never-ending guests.

Heather put the post back in the envelope and tucked the envelope away in her trunk, then gathered her carpetbag and reticule. Taking one last look at her beautiful room, she returned to the kitchen. Dr. Handerhoosen sat at Norman's usual place, still eating.

Hayden stood by the window as if waiting for something. He turned when she entered the room. "Thanks for breakfast, Heather. It was good."

I'm going to miss him. "You're welcome."

"If you're ready, I can take your things out to Doc's buggy."

A lump wedged in her throat. Stiffening her resolve, she nodded. "I'd appreciate that very much."

"Children," Ina whispered, tears filling her eyes. She glanced at the doctor, who was completely focused on his plate. "Won't you two please reconsider? I want what's best for both of you, and I think that's each other." She went over and pulled Hayden by his hand until he was face-to-face with Heather. "What I started, the two of you can finish."

Heather swallowed, listening to the ticking of the clock on the wall. She'd known since her first day that this was how things would end. Now that the time was here, though, it hurt much more than she'd expected. *I refuse to have a husband who has to be roped into marrying me. I'd rather be an old maid for the rest of my life.*

"No, Ina. We understand you had good intentions, but sometimes that just isn't enough. This is for the best. My mind is made up, and so is Hayden's." She looked directly at Hayden so he'd know she was serious. "I don't want to marry you, Hayden. I wouldn't say yes if you were to ask me right now." Her conscience pricked at the white lie needed to release him of any sense of wrongdoing. "I don't want you to think I'm hurt, or pining in any way. I'm not."

"See, Ma." His voice was low, halting. "You can't force things like this. I know you want grandbabies, but this isn't the way to get them. We forgive you, though, don't we, Heather? There's no hard feelings between us."

She longed to reach out and touch his face. Smooth away the worry from his eyes. "No. None at all."

Hayden turned and headed up the stairs to her room, then reappeared with her trunk in his arms. He brought the bulky thing down the staircase and through the house, arms bulging and back straight, careful not to bang any of the walls or knock anything over.

Bittersweet feelings stirred inside Heather. She glanced around the room, memorizing every detail—and especially everything about Hayden. Betrothed or not, she wished she could help him with his situation at the mill. He was a good man. There must be *something* she could do to help. If only her brother Morgan were here. He was an expert at making odd pieces in the hot fire at their blacksmith shop. The frustration on Hayden's face was hard to take. His hands were tied.

"That's it." Hayden stopped in the entry when he came back in, as if needing space between them.

This is good-bye. Her head swam with unspoken words, and her heart thumped wildly.

She nodded, too emotional to say anything.

I'll see him around town, though, she tried to comfort herself.

Turning, he closed the door with a soft click, bringing this part of her adventure to an end.

Chapter Fourteen

Heather nimbly sidestepped a stool in her path, then pushed her way through the swinging door of the boardinghouse, careful not to drop the heavy platter heaped with fried chicken. She hurried forward and set the sizzling fare on the large dining room table, taking in the savory aroma. The tabletop, constructed from a pair of doors nailed together side by side, then set on sawhorses, easily accommodated multiple diners and had room to spare in the middle for the serving dishes of a family-style meal. "Here you are. Anyone interested in a second helping?"

Six sets of eyes riveted on the platter but, as usual, Mr. Slack's fork was first to reach the food. He jabbed a crisp, well-cooked thigh and plopped the piece onto his plate, then reached for the breadbasket. That man had a hollow leg. Lou, owner of the boardinghouse along with her husband, said he'd arrived about three days ago on a mule and playing a mandolin. Lou complained he'd been eating her out of house and home since. If he didn't leave soon, she'd need to increase his board. She didn't clean and cook just to spend more money than she took in.

Then there was the shifty-eyed salesman, always smiling no matter when she looked at him. She'd heard he made a monthly loop between here and Pine Grove, also stopping a few times a year in Grassy Gulch, a small settlement that could hardly be considered a town. He sold everything from knives to blood fortifier. Just being in his presence made Heather vaguely ill at ease. She avoided him whenever possible.

Mrs. Rollins and her two boys were here for a week, visiting relatives. A cattle buyer, just staying the night, was on his way to Wyoming territory and had been scaring little Sip and Tip Rollins with stories about Indian raids and scalping. Mrs. Rollins looked as if she wanted to scalp *him* as her boys quivered and rubbed watery eyes instead of eating their supper.

A dull ache radiated up Heather's back. After three days of working her four jobs, she felt like a worn-out dishrag.

She stood back, her light cotton dress sticking to her perspiring body, and watched the chicken disappear in seconds. With a sigh, she decided in that moment that she'd give her new life three months. If she wasn't happy by then, she'd take herself back to St. Louis and redouble her efforts finding work. She wouldn't stay in Y Knot forever, nursing her hurt feelings and injured pride.

Her new schedule afforded little time to see the beautiful Montana countryside, as she'd dreamt of doing on her trip out in the stagecoach. *How silly I was, envisioning Hayden and me touring the countryside in a shiny black buggy, stopping for a picnic, walking in the moonlight. Silly and naive!*

Ha! Reality was far from her dreams. Rising at five, she helped Drit and Lou with breakfast preparations and cleanup. From there, she was off to Dr. Handerhoosen's office, arriving promptly at eight thirty. There she mostly just washed dirty dishes and straightened up, at least so far. She had removed a wicked splinter for a grateful soldier while Dr. Handerhoosen was away. But that had been the extent of her doctoring tasks. *So much for working in the medical field.*

After two hours in the tiny office, she crossed the street, giving the saloon a wide berth, to go to Berta May's sewing shop. There she cut fabric and hemmed skirts, dresses, and trousers. The tasks Berta May gave her were nothing she couldn't handle. She wished the kindly woman trusted her enough to let her sew a whole dress, as she'd done for herself and sisters more times than she could count. *That* would be gratifying. *All in due time.*

Mr. Lichtenstein employed her for two hours after lunch to go over the inventory and the accounts payable and receivable books. The shopkeeper said he'd never had so much free time on his hands, and as long as she wanted a job, she had employment with him. The mercantile was usually quiet and filled with enticing aromas. Heather enjoyed her time spent there.

From three o'clock until six, she was free. She'd wanted to explore the town, venture out to Evie's house to see the cattle her friend had talked about and meet Dexter, her dog. But since she'd started work, all she could do was go back to her small room on the second floor of the boardinghouse and collapse. She'd sleep until Lou's soft knock on the door told her it was time to get up and help with the evening meal. Somehow, she needed to make time to do her laundry as all her dresses, except for her Sunday best, were soiled. She made a mental note to ask Lou if she could add her clothes to the laundry for the boardinghouse, helping with the whole cleaning process, of course.

Heather heard Drit on the porch speaking with someone, a man by the timbre of his voice, who sounded familiar. Seemed as if Lou's husband was turning the man away. They didn't have a room to spare.

"Excuse me, Heather," Mr. Slack said, bringing her back from her musings. "Can we get another pitcher of milk? This one's plumb dry."

"Yes, of course, Mr. Slack," she replied, taking the glass pitcher from his outstretched hands. "I'll refill it right—"

She turned and looked out the window, trying to see whom Drit was talking to.

"Right down the street, I'm sure Cattlemen's Hotel has a room for you. Tell Mr. Spillmann I—"

Heather gasped. She pushed the milk pitcher back into the hands of the astonished, always-famished boarder, and ran out onto the porch.

"Morgan!"

She stopped and drank in the sight of him; his dark, tousled hair and wide shoulders, perfect for carrying little children; his surprised, half-crooked smile. "Oh, Morgan—" That was all she got out before throwing herself into her older brother's strong, familiar embrace.

Morgan's arms wrapped around her like a protective shield. His beloved scent lifted her spirits and she thanked God in heaven for hearing her prayer. A rush of hot tears pushed up from deep down inside.

"Shhh, now," Morgan crooned. "What're all these tears? Doesn't make me happy to find you like this."

He was solid and steadfast and she didn't want to leave his embrace. Heather remembered the time when she was six and he'd found her crying out behind the blacksmith shop. An older boy from another neighborhood had pushed her down and taken the apple their pa had given her. After drying her tears and giving her his apple, he'd stomped off toward the lout's neighborhood. After that, she'd never had another problem with any of the ruffians who roamed the streets.

When she felt his body stiffen, she opened her eyes to see the boarders crowded in the doorway, craning their necks to see what all the commotion was about. Mrs. Rollins covered her mouth with one pudgy hand, and her boys peered out the window, wide-eyed. Mr. Slack and the cattle buyer were there too.

"Get back inside," Morgan ordered the group, his voice low.

She knew her brother would be giving them a scowl, the one that could quiet a preacher and stop a grizzly in his tracks. "Go on. Do you have cotton stuck in your ears? My sister's not some circus sideshow."

Drit took a step toward the doorway, motioning the boarders inside. "Go on, Mr. Slack, Mrs. Rollins. Go on. Take the kids, too. Give Heather a moment of privacy with her brother."

Heather wiped her eyes with the corner of her apron.

Drit gestured to her and Morgan to sit down in the porch rockers. "Take some time for yourself," he said kindly. "Lou and I can finish up. Don't worry about the dishes, neither. You've been working hard, better than any help we've ever had. I'm sure your brother would like some time with you."

Morgan's face was a mask. "What's this all about?" He picked up his chair, moving with a limp, and brought the rocker close so they wouldn't be overheard. The hitch in his step always broke her heart.

She sniffed once, then took a calming breath. "How'd you find out I didn't marry as planned?" She realized Morgan was wearing Pa's brown plaid shirt and the pants with the hole in the pocket she'd mended the day before she'd packed her trunk and gone to Mrs. Seymour's. The sight brought a fresh round of sentiment.

Angry at herself for being so weak, she dashed the tears away with her hand, knowing Morgan didn't deal well with weepy females. If she didn't pull herself together quickly, he just might give her a not-so-soft buffet on the shoulder to bring her around.

To her utter amazement, Morgan reached up and wiped away a tear she'd missed. He didn't look mad or impatient at all. His warm, sincere gesture touched her deeply.

"I was returning the padre's horse to St. Anthony's Church after a shoeing. On my way, I ran into Lina, hurrying into the church to light a candle for you. She'd just gotten your letter and was sick with worry. Apparently, you'd told her not to tell Mrs. Seymour what was wrong, but you hadn't prohibited her from talking to me. She spilled the tale, sister. And I made all haste to travel out here to you."

The love Heather felt for her dear friend

doubled, then tripled. *Thank goodness Lina saw Morgan, and had the sense to alert him that things were amiss.* Just seeing Morgan's face and hearing his voice brought peace to her heart, peace that had been missing since she'd first arrived in town. She wasn't alone anymore.

"I'm glad she did, because now you're here. First, tell me about home. How is Mother? The family? Melba?"

A shadow crossed Morgan's face.

Heather gripped his arm. "Tell me!"

He shook his head. "No, sis, Melba hasn't died. She's the same, still frail."

Relief flooded through Heather. She looked at her hand resting on his arm, thanking God again that Morgan was now here with her. "How long can you stay?"

"Stay?"

"Before you go home. Back to St. Louis?"

The confident smile she knew so well appeared on his face, making his eyes sparkle in the way that drew women to him like children to blueberry pie. "Who said anything about going back to St. Louis?"

"What! You're not going back? But what about the blacksmith shop?"

"Travis runs the place, and the other boys are there. No need for me to hang around twiddling my thumbs. They'll manage without me."

"Is business really that bad?"

He nodded. "Besides, I've dreamed of the frontier for a long time. If I didn't come now it may be all gone—settled, tamed."

"I never knew you wanted to go west."

"I'd bet there're a lot of things you don't know about me. I understand the reason you signed up at the agency. It wasn't to see the world, or find a husband. You wanted to help Ma and the family. Be one less mouth to feed. I'm doing the same thing. I'm tired of St. Louis. I need some adventure. Do something with my life besides mold horseshoes and mend wagon wheels."

She flung her arms around him again and squeezed him tight.

He gestured to the boardinghouse with his head. "So, what happened to the groom who wrote and asked you to marry him? Hayden Klinkner. I have a mind to teach him a thing or two about messing with my sister."

With the mention of Hayden's name, Heather's thoughts flew back to the lovely home on Creek Street, and she wondered how everyone there was doing. With a start, she realized she'd gotten her desire. Here was Morgan, right before her eyes. Wasn't it just a few days ago she'd been wishing for his help? If anyone could fix Hayden's steam engine, it was her brother. Getting him to agree to it, though, might take some doing.

"It wasn't Hayden's fault."

Morgan's face darkened. "What do you mean? He asked you to marry him, didn't he?"

"Well, actually, no—he didn't ask me."

His nostrils flared. "Don't keep me in suspense, little sister. What're you saying—exactly? I've been dreaming up all the ways this hound will pay for hurting you, for shaming you."

Heat surged to Heather's face. "Hayden didn't write to the agency requesting a mail-order bride. He knew nothing about it." She couldn't look her brother in the eye. Embarrassment for being publicly jilted hurt. "His mother did it. She wanted her son to settle down. So she wrote to me, pretending to be him."

Morgan stood. He limped over to the street side of the porch, looking out at the townspeople, horses, the occasional dog or chicken. "But when you got here," he said over his shoulder, "the man didn't offer to marry you when he found out what his mother had done? To me, that makes his failure worse than her meddling."

Morgan was going to have a hard time understanding.

"No, he didn't," she said, following him to the porch rail. "I arrived right after the engine exploded, injuring his father. Now, he has his father's broken leg to contend with, as well as running the mill and completing a huge order. He has no thoughts of marriage." She stopped and nodded when Dr. Handerhoosen waved to her, his buggy's wheels stirring up the dust on the street.

Morgan cocked his eyebrow. "That Klinkner? He's a bit long in the tooth, don't you think?"

Heather burst into laughter. "No, that's not Hayden." The buggy rattled out of sight. "It's Dr. Handerhoosen, one of my employers."

Morgan arched his other brow cynically, creating a row of lines across his forehead. Since the death of their father, he'd taken his role as protector dead seriously. "Looks sweet on you."

"Not at all." She waved off his concern. "He's kind. I like him."

"That's how things start."

"Morgan! Stop!"

"Fine. I want to talk about Klinkner, anyway. What happened between the two of you?"

"Hayden didn't offer to marry me and I'm glad. I would've had to tell him no. The last thing I'd ever want is to be yoked with someone who didn't really want me. A man who was marrying me out of pity, or duty to his mother, or to me? No, Morgan, I let him know I wanted no part of that."

Morgan straightened. "The Stanford pride. Well and flourishing."

"Perhaps. But there is something I'd like to talk to you about. Something other than me and my problems of late. And time is of the essence."

Morgan turned and leaned his back against the rail, crossing his arms in front of his chest. "Oh? How come I have the feeling I'm about to be talked into something I'll regret?"

Chapter Fifteen

Like it or not, Hayden was aware of Heather's every move since she'd left his parents' house. Everyone thought it was his or her duty to keep him informed. Visitors and customers alike couldn't resist sharing her comings and goings at the boardinghouse, the mercantile, and at the doctor's office. Though the weather was still mild, Berta May, the seamstress, came out to the mill not two days ago with leg warmers for his pa. Her glowing report of the young woman from St. Louis had his ma and pa beaming as if Heather were their own daughter.

He was tired of it. Didn't want to hear another word about the woman. Actually, her memory had kept him awake almost every night, leaving him cranky and frustrated in the mornings. Just when he needed a clear head.

Hayden groaned inwardly when he saw Dr. Handerhoosen's buggy pull up in front of the house. The silly grin on the man's face meant he was about to share some wonderful tale about Heather. She was widely regarded as the Mail-Order Bride Done Wrong. And as much as he tried to explain the circumstances, everyone believed he was the one who had done the wronging.

Hell! I'm not guilty!

The more he talked, the narrower people's eyes became. In exasperation, he kicked the log next to him.

Ralph Hicks, one of the lumberjacks who sold him timber, looked his way. "Something wrong?"

"Nope," he lied. "Not a dad-burned thing."

As the doctor climbed out of his buggy and headed up the walk to the main house, Hayden bit the inside of his lip. He felt as out of sorts as a wet porcupine.

Ralph, dressed in overalls and black boots, unhitched the heavy chain releasing two of his four-horse draft team from the group of logs he'd just dragged from the riverbank, then unhitched the other two from behind. "That frown on your face says different. Don't you like the logs?"

"Of course I like the logs. You and Jed have always supplied the mill. Why wouldn't I like them now?"

The man shrugged and led the two lead chestnuts, their flaxen manes rippling in the breeze, over to the water trough. The huge Belgians plunged their large muzzles into the trough, sucking the cold water into their mouths. Steam radiated from their sweaty hides.

Ralph pulled them away after a moment, not wanting them to drink too much water while they were still hot. "Fine, then. I'll be back with the next load in about an hour."

Hayden placed his foot on the nearest pine log and watched Ralph water the other two, then lead the team back down the narrow logging road, the chain rattling behind in the dust.

He turned at the sound of more wagon wheels.

Busier here today than the pie line at the Christmas social.

Irritated at the little work he'd accomplished, it took him several moments before he recognized Heather, in overalls and a hat, sitting on the buckboard seat next to a stranger. A sickening jolt of jealousy flashed through his body, and he didn't miss the scowl on the driver's face. Intuition told him this didn't bode well.

Heather's sour-faced escort drew the team to a halt at the mill and set the brake. He climbed out of the wagon, then limped around to the other side to help Heather down.

"Hayden," Heather said as the two approached. "This is Morgan, my brother from St. Louis."

So, that's how she's playing it. Reinforcements from home. Hayden extended his hand, and for one instant thought the brother wasn't going to take it.

Morgan stood eye to eye with him, radiating disdain. Then he gripped Hayden's hand fiercely, no doubt showing him just what he thought of his treatment of Heather. "Klinkner," he said through clenched teeth.

Hayden gave back as good as he got.

A small furrow appeared between Heather's eyes as she watched the exchange. She cleared her throat. "Boys, *please,*" she said, stomping one boot-clad foot.

Her brother, his mouth a straight, hard line, let go first.

Hayden resisted the urge to shake some blood back into his extremity.

Heather sighed in relief. Smiling, she asked, "How's your father?"

He didn't want to admit to himself just how pretty she looked, even in her strange attire. "Doing better. Been up and moving around with the crutches Doc brought out yesterday. I hear you're working for Doc. Good. Keep you out of trouble." *Whoa, where did that come from?*

Morgan leaned forward and growled.

Hayden made a mental note to be more careful with what he said. He wasn't afraid of a fight, but right now, with the mill shut down, he had more important things to do than show this city boy how a country boy could whip his hind end. "Doc's checking him out right now."

Heather wondered at Hayden's anger. His edginess was evident in his stance, the way he carried his body. "I'm happy to hear that. Dr. Handerhoosen keeps me abreast of his daily progress. It's good to know there's no more danger of infection."

Hayden turned and walked toward the mill. Over his shoulder he said, "What did you come to say, Heather? I'm sure your trip out wasn't just to exchange niceties. Or acquaint me with your family. Get to the point. I'm a busy man."

Shocked at his rudeness, Heather fought embarrassment. *What's wrong with him? Why is he being so rude?* She'd worked hard on her brother to get him to agree to help Hayden. Firmly opposed to the idea, Morgan had argued for a good thirty minutes why he didn't want to do it. And from his perspective, she could understand why. If it weren't for Ina and Norman, she might turn right around and leave Hayden to his troubles.

"Come on, Heather. Get in the wagon. It's plain he doesn't want our help."

Hayden turned around.

Heather glanced toward the steam engine. "We've come to help you fix your equipment, Hayden. Get the mill up and running. In St. Louis, no one was better than Morgan at making tricky objects in our smithy. He's offered his services to help you while your father is incapacitated. He's offered to help mill the Night Owl order too."

Hayden dropped his gaze to her overalls. "Is that why you're dressed like a man?"

She nodded, still feeling sad that everything had come to this. "Yes. My employers gave me a couple of days off so I could help, too. Lou had a few things her youngest boy grew out of." She gestured to her overalls. "Anyway, let Morgan take a look, and then we'll go back to the livery in town and get started."

"June Pittman's gone."

"I know. Jack's watching the place since the sheriff's office is directly across the street. I asked him and he said we could use her forge."

His face hardened. "You have this all figured out, don't you?"

"Not really, Klinkner," Morgan said, crossing his arms. The muscle in his jaw worked several times.

Heather prepared herself for the worst.

"If you don't want our help, just say so," her brother snapped. "We'll be *happy* to leave you to your work."

Morgan made it clear he didn't like Hayden. And why should he? She didn't like him much right now either.

Hayden glanced at the steam engine some ten feet away. He flexed his shoulders. "No. You're wrong. I'd be obliged for the help."

Morgan's mouth was still a rigid line. "You can be obliged all you want. That doesn't mean I like you any better. I'm only doing this for my sister, and her devotion to anyone or any*thing* that needs help."

Morgan was being tenacious and Heather wished he'd stop. Hayden had softened, and she wished Morgan would, too. But his stubborn streak was as wide as the Mississippi back home. It would be days, if ever, before the hard edge of his resentment began to yield.

Hayden nodded. "I understand, Stanford. And I guess I don't really blame you." He started for the contraption. "Come over here and take a look. I've been trying to figure out how this happened. It's been functioning just fine for years. I won't say the machine hasn't had a problem now and then, but nothing like this. It's almost as if it were intentional. And if it was, I'd sure like to get my hands on the person who almost killed my pa."

Morgan pretended to be studying the house, but Heather knew he couldn't wait to get over there and dirty his hands on the damaged machinery. She'd seen the look often when Travis had something of interest to show Morgan, but kept it just out of his grasp.

With a grunt, Morgan stuffed his hands in his pockets and followed after Hayden.

Heather stood back as the two men marched off as if they'd been friends forever. Fancy that. Amazing how something as mundane as a steam engine could draw them out of their anger.

"Over here," Hayden said, leading Morgan around to the contraption's other side. They vanished from sight, and several moments passed before Hayden stuck his head over the top and called to her, "Aren't you coming, Heather?

I hear you're darn good at the smithy, too."

"Yes. Just as soon as I go in and say hello to Ina and Norman. It's been a while since we've seen each other and I have so much to tell them."

Hayden nodded.

She thought she saw a light come back into his eyes, a softening of his mouth. When her heart quickened, she reminded herself that things hadn't changed. He wasn't interested in a wife. She'd do well to remember that!

Chapter Sixteen

Evie put her hands on Chance's broad shoulders and he lifted her out of the buckboard in front of the boardinghouse. Once on the ground, she hurried up the stone walkway. She knocked on the door. When no one answered, she opened it and took a step inside. "Hello?"

The house was quiet. Everyone must be gone or getting ready for Sunday service. When a melodic strumming began, Evie turned and looked down the hallway that ran under the stairs.

A man came into the front room, a mandolin in his hands. "Why, hello, young lady," he said as he strummed. "Can I help ya?"

Surprised at first, Evie didn't know how to respond. In Mrs. Seymour's library she'd read accounts of traveling musicians, but he was the first one she'd ever encountered. His close-fitting vest was threadbare; a string tie and a well-worn black stovetop hat completed his ensemble.

"I—I'm here to pick up my friend, Heather Stanford, for church."

"Here I am," Heather called as she stepped quickly down the stairs, her boots clipping merrily to the tune. "I'm so excited to spend time with you and Chance this morning. I've looked forward to our visit all week." She looked at the raggedy man. "Have the two of you met?"

Evie smiled. "No, not officially. But I've been enjoying his music."

The musician's nimble fingers never stopped as he started another jaunty tune:

> *I'm Casper Slack, a minstrel by trade.*
> *I'll sing for my supper, whatever you've made.*
> *One day I'm here, and the next I'll be gone.*
> *If you've time on your hands, I'll sing you a song.*

Evie looked at Heather and both women burst into laughter. Heather looked beautiful, much happier than she'd been when Evie first spoke with her at Ina's. Her yellow chiffon dress flowed gently when she moved, and her hair was brushed to a high sheen. Even with all the chores she'd been doing, she looked rested. "Shall we go?" Evie asked between giggles. "Chance is waiting in the wagon."

"He is? Of course! I don't want to keep him waiting. I thought we were walking or I'd have been down sooner."

"It's a pleasure to meet you, Mr. Slack. I hope to hear more of your music," Evie said, turning to go.

Before they could get out the door, a racket

erupted on the staircase, then two boys appeared, laughing and poking elbows into each other's sides. They both had slicked-back hair and pressed collared shirts that left little doubt they were headed to the same place as Evie and Heather.

"Keep the noise down, boys!" a female voice called from the second floor. "A locomotive is quieter than the two of you rascals."

The boys ducked their heads and darted out the door, cutting in front of Heather and Evie, almost tripping them.

Evie took Heather's hand as they hurried for the buckboard. "I can't tell you how happy I am you're here in Y Knot, Heather," Evie said. "Even though the town is rustic, it has everything you might need or want. The people are nice and helpful. Everything is going to work out just fine. You'll see." *I sincerely hope Heather finds the happiness I have with Chance. I can't even remember life without him.*

Chance was speaking with Jack Jones at the side of the wagon. Both men turned as the women approached. Evie had the distinct impression the deputy had been waiting for Heather to appear from the boardinghouse.

"Good day, Deputy," Evie said, taking Chance's hand.

"Good day, Mrs. Holcomb."

Chance helped her up to the seat. When she

was comfortable, her husband turned. "Jack has offered to walk you to the church, Heather. I told him you were in my charge today, and the decision was up to you."

Heather's eyes locked on to Evie's. Evie could see her friend's indecision. She was sure Heather had feelings for Hayden—just sure of it! But Heather hadn't said so, and her pride had been deeply hurt in the face of the circumstances with the letters.

Y Knot was small. A woman didn't go from one man to the next. Courtship was taken seriously—and could brand her as the deputy's girl. It would be a mistake if Heather was waiting for Hayden. She really couldn't blame Hayden for pulling back. All this had happened so fast. He needed some time to warm up to the idea of settling down. No one was going to force that man.

"Thank you, Deputy, but I—"

"Call me Jack."

"All right, Jack. Thank you for your offer, but I've been looking forward to spending time with my friend Evie. I'd be remiss to relinquish even a moment of it."

She smiled, then looked at Chance, who reached out to help her up beside Evie.

Evie breathed a sigh of relief. *The right choice.*

Now that she'd had a few days to think it over, Hayden would be a perfect match for Heather. Where Heather was serious, Hayden's playful side could lighten the days. Moreover, where Hayden's mind sometimes wandered, Heather was strong, resilient, determined. No man would get the best of her for long! She'd met two of Heather's brothers back in St. Louis. Any girl growing up with brothers like that had to be a tiny bit tough.

A new respect for Mrs. Seymour, and how she matched couples together, blossomed in Evie's chest. Love for the woman who'd been like a stepmother warmed her heart.

Evie sat a little straighter as the wagon rolled through Y Knot and toward the little hill where the townsfolk gathered at the church. She'd just had an all-important task, a life's happiness, handed to her. There was something special between Heather and Hayden. A kind of connection that came along only once in a great while. With Mrs. Seymour back in St. Louis, it would be up to her to make sure this perfect match was made!

The morning passed too quickly. Evie introduced Heather to everyone she could before and after the service. When they dropped Heather at the boardinghouse, Evie regretted their time together had come to an end.

Thank heavens she wasn't in Heather's shoes! Every man, married or not, had been overly curious about the new mail-order bride done wrong. They'd tried to be discreet, but one male or another had turned, craned their necks—or stared outright. How irritating. She'd felt Chance stiffen more than a few times. The sooner Hayden wised up, the better for the whole town.

And this was the first time she'd ever seen Jack Jones grace the inside of the blue church. She had to clamp her mouth closed when he claimed he never missed a service. He should be ashamed for spinning untruths. If a man lied about small things, you could bet he lied about the big ones, too. *And how foolish of him. Didn't he think she'd fill Heather in on the truth as soon as he was out of earshot?*

"You're awful quiet, Evie," Chance said, driving the horses back toward the ranch. They'd just passed the mail drop at the big tree. Whenever Evie traveled this part of the road, a warm and wonderful feeling blossomed inside her. This was where Chance had first kissed her for real, then took her home and made her his own. "Something bothering you?"

"Not just one something, but several."

"Oh?"

"I'm just thinking about Heather and how she has to make her way now that she and Hayden aren't getting married. She hasn't said so, but I know she's working very hard. She misses her family, especially her youngest sister, Melba. Have I told you about her being sick?"

Chance nodded. "You have."

"Well, Heather's worried about her. The doctors don't know what's wrong but she keeps getting weaker. One day they fear she'll just go to sleep and not wake up."

Fluffy clouds filled the sky, keeping the hot sun at bay. She'd become accustomed to the vast, rolling hills, void of people and the bustle of St. Louis. She could never go back. This country was as different from St. Louis as from the moon.

"That's a shame."

Evie reached for Chance's arm and hugged it close, thinking how blessed she was.

He smiled and flipped the reins, hurrying the horses along.

"Yes, it is. And now, on top of that, it's not fair that she has to worry about making ends meet, too, as well as fending off all the bachelors that will be coming to her door. I know she has feelings for Hayden. But I fear he's a lost cause."

"Has she said as much?"

"Not exactly."

"Evie." The warning tone in her husband's voice made her look out at the land to avoid his assessment.

Chance took his finger and turned her face so he could look into her eyes.

"Evie, do you know for a fact she has feelings for Hayden, or are you making that up because it's what you want? You're good friends with Ina.

It's no secret how she'd like to see Hayden settle down. I don't think it's wise you gettin' in the middle of this. Maybe Hayden isn't the right man for her. You know how I feel about him."

"She didn't say so, but the other night, when we talked at Ina's, I saw something in her eyes, heard it in her voice. She's fallen in love with him, but won't admit to it."

He grunted.

She glanced up at Chance's profile, his attention now back on driving the wagon. Thankfulness that things had worked out for the two of them filled her. The thought of spending her life without Chance was heartbreaking.

"Chance?"

"Yes," he said, turning the team at the split in the road. They were almost home. She was glad. The rocking motion of the wagon had her feeling a little woozy.

"What is it *exactly* that you don't like about Hayden? You'd said you thought I went over to Ina's to see him, and that you were jealous. But seemed to me it was more than just jealousy. Is there more? Something you haven't told me?"

Chance was quiet so long Evie gave his leg a squeeze.

"Tell me. He's never really been that flirtatious with me. Maybe smiled a little too long, but once he knew we were married, he hasn't made any advances. It's his personality to be playful."

"Playful!"

Is Chance's face actually turning red? "Chance?"

"I don't want to be talking about the man behind his back, Evie. Don't ask me to do that."

"It's not like I want to gossip. It's for a good purpose. If you have some reason you don't like him, other than that he's handsome and—"

Chance cast her an annoyed expression.

She stiffened her spine. "Well, he is. The man can't help the way he looks. If you really don't think they should marry, say so now."

Chance cleared his throat, as if deciding how much he should say. "A few years back there was talk about him and another man's wife over in Pine Grove. No one really knew what happened, but I believe she left town."

"She left her husband?" Surprised, Evie sat back, thinking. "And nobody knows why? Her husband didn't say?"

Chance removed his hat and jammed his fingers through his hair, a clear sign to Evie he was near his breaking point. This was a touchy subject for them, but since they'd gotten everything straightened out weeks ago, and their marriage was all it should be, and so much more—at least in her eyes, he shouldn't have difficulty talking about Hayden anymore. Chance knew how much she adored him. She lived for his smile, the way he made her laugh, the feel of his work-roughened hands on her skin.

The wagon wheel dipped in a gopher hole. She grasped the side of the seat at the same time they heard Dexter's excited welcome-home bark.

"Like I said before, no one really knows, and Hayden wasn't saying. Ask him yourself if it means that much to you."

"Besides that incident, is there any other reason you don't like him?"

"Whoa, now," he called to the horses in front of the house.

Dexter ran around and jumped in the back of the wagon. He trotted forward and licked Evie's face before she knew what he was up to.

Chance turned, slinging his arm across the back of the seat.

"One," he said, an angry edge to his voice, "he talks too damn much. Two, I didn't like the way he flirted with Faith when she first came to Y Knot. Three, the situation in Pine Grove I mentioned before. Four, every time I go for lumber he has to contradict everything I say . . ."

Laughing, she wiped off Dexter's kiss. "All right, all right, I understand. You two are like oil and water. I won't question that again. But . . ."

Without another word, Chance stepped out of the wagon and looked at the barn.

Boston's head went up from the other side of the corral and he nickered to his friends in the harness.

"Isn't that enough? My God, woman, don't you know when to quit?"

She had to have this all out now, so she'd know how to proceed. So they wouldn't have to revisit the topic later—and make him upset all over again.

"Yes, Chance, I do. And I promise you, I'm almost finished. But as I was about to ask, is there some *real* reason you don't like him? Besides that incident you mentioned in Pine Grove. Maybe that woman wanted to leave her husband, and he helped her? I don't know. There could be lots of reasons we don't know about. No, the more I think about it, I'm sure I shouldn't pry. That was years ago. I'll not mention anything to Heather. What's in the past is best left in the past. We've all done things we wished later we hadn't."

"You know, Evie, this has been a fine day—up till now. Think I'll go saddle Boston and take him for a nice long ride. It's been a while since he's been out."

She gasped. "Chance?" Perhaps she'd pushed him too far.

Chance strode toward the barn, halting for a moment to call over his shoulder, "I'll see you at supper."

Chapter Seventeen

"Let's try this one more time," Morgan said. He dismounted, then tied the horse he'd borrowed from one of June's stalls to the hitching rail.

The gelding cocked his hind fetlock and got comfortable.

Morgan headed for the steam engine, holding an intricate, three-inch-square patch he'd made and brought in from the blacksmith's shop only moments ago. He stopped and studied the blown hole once again.

Hayden nodded, thankful that Heather's brother had shown up in Y Knot when he did—and had agreed to help. The two of them had gotten more done these last three days than he had all last week. Ralph and Jed Hicks had delivered several more loads of logs, giving them almost enough for half the Night Owl order.

This was their second try with the patch. If the machine didn't hold steam, enough to turn the belt that ran the saw, he'd have to ride over tonight and talk with Stef Hannessy. The news about his pa had traveled to Pine Grove. Hannessy had sent a note by carrier yesterday inquiring if they were going to be able to deliver the lumber on time. If everything proceeded smoothly from here, with no more complications, they should be able to do it. *I'll move heaven and earth to make this order happen!*

Morgan jimmied the metal patch. It needed to cover a port, but was too large, affecting a port that had not been damaged. He tried again, with the same results.

"Maybe try a little more to the left," Hayden suggested, pressing his cheek on the cold iron in an effort to see. "Looks like your angle isn't quite right."

Morgan pulled back. He rubbed his fingers together for a brief moment, as if getting ready to crack a bank safe, then tried again. Unable to get the piece installed, he took it out and studied the edge. "Still just a bit off," he said. "Would be a whole lot easier if your mill was closer to town. I'll go back to the smithy, shave a little off."

Hayden walked with him to his horse. He expected Ralph Hicks with the next haul of logs, or else he'd go with him.

"Thanks, Morgan. Can't tell you how much this means to us. I wish I was more familiar with the thing, but my pa usually won't let anyone else near his precious engine."

"You've thanked me enough," Morgan replied, taking his horse's reins.

Should I ask? He didn't want to reopen a still-ugly wound, but curiosity got the better of him. "Heather couldn't make it today?"

"No. She has obligations. One thing about my

sister, she takes her promises seriously. She has work to do."

Touché. I walked right into that.

Morgan mounted, a dark glint in his eyes. Up until now, they'd reached a truce. But now . . . "I do think, though, she's saved a little time to see that new feller that stopped by the boardinghouse Sunday evening."

"New? You mean Jack Jones, the deputy?"

"No. She has more sense than to pin her future on a man like that. Roady Guthrie. Works for some large outfit around here. I'm sure you've heard of it."

Roady!

"Seems like a solid fellow. Liked the man the minute I met him. I think Heather's taken a shine to him, too. Offered to take her out to the Holcombs' for a visit next Thursday evening when she's finished with work." He reined his horse around. "Good to see a smile back on her face."

Roady Guthrie! The thought of the cowboy courting Heather still hurt. Why it should, Hayden didn't know. He leaned his forearms on the bar top and waited for Abe to come down and pour him a beer. He was sweaty and tired from work and had offered to buy Morgan a drink. Heather's brother had gotten the patch successfully installed on the third try. As soon as he stabled his horse at June's, he'd be in. The Night Owl job should be all downhill from here.

"About time you came to see me," Fancy said, sidling up next to him. She leaned her elbows back against the bar, giving Hayden an eyeful of her curvaceous figure before he knew what she was up to.

He glanced away. "Sorry, Fancy, been real busy out at the mill."

"Why the long face?"

Fancy was good-hearted, but he wished he could just stand here in peace, without getting a hundred questions thrown his way.

When he didn't answer, the saloon girl shrugged. "Heard your gal's seeing Roady."

News travels fast!

Abe set a foamy beer on the bar top, then walked away, leaving them to their conversation.

"She's not my girl, Fancy, and you know it. And by now, the whole town knows it, too. I never sent for her! What does everyone expect me to do, marry a stranger?"

"That's the whole idea behind being a mail-order bride, sugar. She was willing to wed you, *a stranger.* You might like marriage if you gave it a try."

His face heated.

Seeing his reaction, Fancy held up her hand. "Cool down, love. I didn't mean to rile you."

Hayden took a long pull on his beer, letting the hops' bitter bite soothe his temper. Meanwhile, his relief over getting the engine fixed was all but gone. He'd seen the censure in Mr. Lichtenstein's eyes this afternoon, as well as Mr. Herrick's when he'd gone into the leather shop for a new set of reins.

A burst of laughter from the back of the bar made him shake his head, thinking the men were probably joking about him.

"Well, you did. And I think you meant to. Everyone in town is treating me like I'm some kind of leper. Like I purposely sent for Heather just so I could reject her, hurt her."

"All right, all right. Let's change the subject. How's your pa doing? Feeling better?"

"He's up and about, with the help of my ma, that is, and some crutches. It'll be a while before he's dancing a jig."

"I hear Morgan Stanford's working with you at the mill."

"You've met?" Hayden forced a chuckle. "Of course you have. And why aren't I surprised. For someone so new in town, seems you know everyone and everything that goes on around here much better than I do. I'm gonna start asking *you* questions."

She lifted a shoulder and smiled, her perfume lingering. For one instant a lost-little-girl look flitted across her face.

"I guess I do, now that you mention it. But a gal needs something to pass the time in a boring cow town like this."

He hadn't meant to be so harsh.

"Besides," Fancy continued. "I think this young woman, this Heather Stanford, is under your skin. Like it or not, sugar, once that happens, there's no turning back—no cure of the thing that ails you." She lifted a brow when he looked her way. "She's pretty. I like her."

"Wouldn't make a difference if I did like her. She has no interest in me. Made it clear since learning I hadn't sent for her. Said she's changed her mind and wouldn't marry me if I asked." He chuckled again, trying not to sound bitter. "Yep. She's let me off the hook."

"Maybe. Maybe not. You might be surprised." Fancy glanced at the large clock hanging over the bar. "Let me know if you change *your* mind and need a pretty face to make her jealous. I'll be happy to oblige."

"Fancy!" a voice boomed from the back of the room. "We're thirsty! Bring another bottle of whiskey."

Her smile faded and her chin jutted out defensively. "Nice passing the time with you."

That got him in the gut. Hayden regretted his angry words. *What must her life be like?* He watched as she slowly approached the table of drunken men, a bottle of whiskey in her hands.

When inebriated laughter rang out again, he turned back to the bar to stare into his half-empty mug.

Would settling down really be so bad? He wanted to, for his ma's sake. Make her happy. But even if he did, he'd never be able to go back and give his ma what he'd taken from her, even if it wasn't his fault.

He blinked, a pain edging into his heart. The ache came with the memory of a long-ago conversation, one he'd overheard while hidden away the night before Christmas.

His mother had put him to bed hours before and must have thought him fast asleep. But he wasn't. He was under the staircase, waiting up to see St. Nick. Wrapped in the blanket from his bed, he'd almost nodded off when he heard a sound on the porch. Pulling back so he'd not be seen, Hayden had spied his mother running to the door and opening it to his father, who carried in a red sled.

It took a moment for the meaning of the scene to sink in. Burying his face in the blanket so they wouldn't hear him sniffling, Hayden began to cry. His friends were right. St. Nick was just someone parents made up.

"It's beautiful, Norman," his ma had whispered. "Hayden is going to love it."

"I hope so. That boy's been asking for a sled

for a good two years. I think he's old enough now to handle it without hurting himself."

Hayden peeked through the stairs. Watched his parents embrace, kiss. His mother placed her head on his father's shoulder as they looked at the tiny pine tree decorated with small white candles.

When his mother started to cry, he wanted to run from his hiding place and apologize for peeking, for ruining Christmas. Why was she crying? Did she know he was watching? He got to his knees and prepared to leave his hiding place. Then his mother said the words that would stop him and change his world forever.

"I wish every year at Christmas for a miracle, for God to change the past."

His pa stroked her hair. "Shhh, Ina. I know. I do, too. But we have Hayden. He's a good son. We're blessed."

What did he mean? Hayden didn't understand. Now he wished he could get back to bed where Ma had put him, tucked him in, and kissed his forehead. Something inside him said he didn't want to know what was coming next. But now it couldn't be helped.

"If only Hayden's birth had been easier," she whispered. "If only he'd been early instead of late. He'd have been smaller and—"

"Hush, now," Pa said gently. "We've had this conversation. Doesn't help a thing."

"Maybe then we'd have five more children to fill this house with laughter. Maybe then . . ."

"Shhh . . . wishing and thinking aren't going to change a thing. What's done is done."

A burst of braying laughter brought Hayden out of the painful memory. His throat, as tight as a shrunken rope, burned. His lungs felt full of sand. He grabbed for his mug, took a swig. That's why his ma pushed him at every girl that looked his way. She craved what he'd robbed her of without even knowing it. He'd never told her he'd overheard them that snowy night. He carried the scar inside like a wound of war. He hadn't understood what they'd meant for the longest time.

Then, when he grew up, learned the ways of men and women, he realized he'd hurt her in some way that kept her from having more children. A bitter pill for someone who yearned for a large family. Why didn't he just give in? Make her happy? Atone for what he'd caused? That was something he couldn't figure out.

The bar doors swung open. Expecting Morgan, Hayden was surprised when Roady walked in. Lucky followed, as well as Francis and Pedro, all ranch hands at the McCutcheon ranch. His friends approached.

Roady tossed a couple of silver dollars onto the bar. "This round's on me, Abe," he called down to the bartender. "I'm celebrating."

"Coming right up."

Hayden just looked at Roady. He had no call to be mad at him. *None!* But by golly, he felt ticked off.

Roady took a long draw on the foamy brew Abe set in front of him. "Guess you heard."

"Heard what?" He felt outnumbered. That was foolish. These were his friends, not his enemies.

"That Roady's taking Heather out for a ride Thursday evening," Francis tossed in. The boy had downed half his beer and was smacking his lips. "Said he saw her when she arrived in Y Knot her first day. Saw her in Lichtenstein's, *before* Jack Jones met her on the boardwalk. Luke was there. He'll vouch for him. That gives him—"

"Francis, my amigo," Pedro said quietly. "Best walk softly, *sí?*"

The look of amusement in the Mexican's black eyes made Hayden bristle.

He needed to keep his cool. He grinned, probably too wide to seem sincere. "That right?"

Lucky leaned in, as if not wanting to be left out of the teasing. "Hayden has no reason to be mad, Francis."

"That's right," Roady said, his cocky smile splitting his face. "I'm doing him an enormous favor by taking Heather off his hands, thus seeing that he keeps his bachelorhood intact."

Lucky nodded. "Right as rain, Roady. Won't be long before everyone stops calling her

Mail-Order-Bride-Done-Wrong, and renames her Mail-Order-Bride-Done-*Right!*"

The group of men howled with laughter. Roady slapped Lucky on the back. "Hey, I like that. I'm remembering that one."

Hayden bit the inside of his cheek until he tasted blood. *These are my friends! They're only having fun—if at my expense. I can handle it. If I react, it'll just encourage them.*

Several more cowboys burst through the saloon doors, livening the place up even more. Morgan entered, too. Hayden looked around. Anxious to change the subject before he did something he'd regret—like pummel Roady's face in jealousy—Hayden called to Morgan.

Heather's brother nodded and headed their way.

Chapter Eighteen

The next evening arrived without fanfare. The chill of the twilight settled over the land as Hayden's buckboard rolled down Main Street. Before giving himself a chance to chicken out, he reined the horses to a stop in front of Drit and Lou's boardinghouse and pushed on the brake. As he hopped out, he glanced quickly up and down the street. Y Knot was quiet. Most people had gone in for supper.

On the porch, he stopped. Removed his hat. Should he knock? He'd never knocked before. This was a boardinghouse. People just walked in and out. But this felt different. Heather was in there. He lifted his hand to knock, then thought better of it. Opening the door, he stepped inside.

Heather was setting the table. A look of astonishment crossed her face as she recognized him. Sadness made his chest ache. He'd seen her like this in his own kitchen, setting the table, mixing the gravy until there were no lumps. And tending to his family—people she'd just met—as if they were her own kin.

As if in a dream, he crossed the floor without conscious awareness. Suddenly he was in front of her. "Heather." The memory of Roady and the others last night in the bar tried to intrude.

She waited. Darted a nervous look at the door.

"I wondered if you'd like to take a ride out to Chance and Evie's with me. I have the lumber for their henhouse. Have had it since the day before the accident but haven't had a chance to deliver it. Evie's anxious to get the coop built and get some chickens. Thought you might like . . ."

He was babbling. Why the heck had he stopped here? She didn't want to go with him. He shrugged and closed his mouth, deciding not to say another word until she gave him his answer.

"Tonight? Right now?" She glanced at the table and then to the forks she held in her hand.

Lou came through the door, wiping her hands on a dishtowel. The front of her apron was damp and spotted.

"Well, Hayden, hello. What can we do for you?" she asked, looking between them. "Supper's almost on. Would you like to join us? We have plenty."

Something about this whole situation made him feel ten years old, with his first crush.

"No, thank you, Lou. I came to see if Heather would like to ride out with me to deliver some lumber to the Holcomb Ranch. It's a nice evening."

Damn. His face must be three shades of red. Some man came down the hall playing on a beat-up old mandolin. He stopped when he saw Hayden, a curious look on his face.

"Well, what do you say?" he said dryly. Then looked around. He was ready to give up on this whole thing and bolt for the door.

A smile broke out on Lou's face. "I think that's a wonderful idea, Hayden. Heather has been working her little fingers to the knucklebone."

Lou hurried over and took the forks from Heather's hands. Some womanly look passed between the two, but he didn't know what it meant. If Heather was coming, he wished she'd say so.

Lou pushed her toward the stairs. "Go on now, girl. Get your shawl. It'll get cold on your ride home."

Hayden passed his hat between his hands as he watched Heather ascend the stairs.

The mandolin man came forward and put out his hand. "I'm Casper Slack, new to town."

Hayden grasped it, remembering that he'd seen the man riding a mule on the road to the mill the day before the accident. Was it possible he had something to do with it? "Hayden Klinkner."

Surprise registered in the man's eyes. "You're *him*. The man." He hooked a thumb toward the way Heather had gone up the stairs. "The one that—"

"Hayden runs the mill here in town with his pa," Lou interjected. "The Klinkners have been providing Y Knot with lumber for many years."

He'd remember to thank her later.

The door opened and Drit came through carrying a basket containing a few tomatoes, an onion, a loaf of bread, and a few letters.

" 'Bout time you got back," Lou said in a scolding tone. "I need those vegetables."

He passed her the basket.

"What are these?" she asked, noticing the letters.

"Mail. From the mercantile."

"What?" Lou's eyes opened wide. "We don't get mail except at Christmastime. What could this be about?"

"Not for us," Drit corrected. "Mr. Simpson just asked me to bring them down. He woulda delivered them himself since they're so many, but his knee's been acting up something awful."

Lou picked up one, holding it out as if were a rattler ready to strike. "Mail-Order Bride, General Delivery, Y Knot." She looked at Hayden.

He swallowed, held her gaze.

She took the next. "Mail-Order Girl, Lichtenstein's Provisions, Y Knot. Mail-Order Bride, General Delivery. Miss Mail-Order Bride, Y Knot General Delivery."

Shaking her head in disbelief, she stopped reading and flipped quickly through the remainder, which looked to be about ten. "All for the mail-order bride. We know who that is."

Drit scratched his head, looking befuddled.

Hayden kept his mouth shut. Shifting his weight, he wished Heather would hurry up.

"What's it all about?" Drit finally said. "Who're they from?"

Lou looked again. "I'll not give the personal names away, of course, because that ain't none of our business—but one's from Y Knot, one's from Pine Grove." A slow smile blossomed over her face. "Y Knot, Pine Grove, Y Knot, Pine Grove. Seems the news about Heather has gotten out. That gal will have her pick of husbands. Most likely, there'll be more to come, too."

The room felt twenty degrees hotter.

"No, wait!" Lou's eyes opened wide in sympathy. "Here's one for Heather Klinkner!" She clucked her tongue like a distraught mother hen. "From Sally Stanford in St. Louis." Her brows tented up. "Oh, the poor thing. That's her younger sister. Seems Heather hasn't sent the embarrassing news home yet."

Lou flipped to the next. Bringing the letter to her nose, she inhaled appreciatively. "A gal after my own heart—smells like fresh garlic. She's not taking a chance of getting the address wrong. She addressed it to Heather Stanford or Heather Klinkner! From Lina Napolitano, in St. Louis."

Drit took the post from Lina Napolitano and smelled it. "You're right about that, Lou! Simpson sure earned his wage today with all these posts. I swear . . ."

The musician, probably thinking he was being funny, started up a jaunty tune on his mandolin.

When Heather came down the stairs, shawl and reticule in hand, her hair was combed and it looked as if she'd freshened up. Hayden was just waiting for one of the group to shout out the good news of all her suitors. To his surprise, they all kept quiet.

She stopped as she stepped off the last stair. Her eyes narrowed. "What? You all look strange."

Lou, still holding the loot, held them out to her.

Heather's eyes grew round. She took envelopes, some dirty, some bent, and glanced at the first, the second. She swallowed, looked up at him from under her lashes. "I'll be right back," she said, turning to the stairs.

He watched her go. What was she going to do, leave him here feeling like the town fool, to cool his heels?

She was back within moments.

Without another teasing word from Drit or Lou, Hayden opened the door for Heather, wondering again what had possessed him to do such a thing as stop and ask her out. Roady Guthrie came to mind. No, he wasn't that much of a cad, was he?

At the wagon, he handed Heather up. The musician came out on the porch and watched them go. Hayden glanced back at the house as the soft strains of "Sweet Betsy From Pike" wafted out to the wagon.

> Oh don't you remember sweet Betsy from Pike,
> Who crossed the wide prairie with her lover, Ike,
> With two yoke of oxen, a big yellow dog,
> A tall Shanghai rooster, and one spotted hog?
>
> One evening quite early they camped on the Platte.
> 'Twas near by the road on a green shady flat.
> Where Betsy, sore-footed, lay down to repose—
> With wonder Ike gazed on that Pike County rose.

Hayden slapped the reins over the horses and started off. Heather hadn't said a word and he wondered what she was thinking. They passed Lark Foot's Street, with all the cozy homes, then the little blue church on the hill. First one cricket started up, followed by two, then four. By the time they reached the edge of town, a whole chorus was chirping away and all the shadows had disappeared. It wouldn't be long before an early star or two appeared.

When Heather drew her shawl closer around her shoulders, he took the opportunity to break the ice. "Chilly?"

"Maybe a little. Feels nice, though, to get out of the house."

"It must. I hear you've been working pretty hard." Why shouldn't she? She had to support herself now that he'd jilted her.

"Not any more than the next person."

He liked her voice. The medium pitch was a bit unusual for a woman, but it was smooth, calm. And best of all, it didn't hold any of the condemnation he'd been getting from everyone else.

"How's your father?"

"Good. Thanks for asking. He's hobbling around with the help of my mother—when she lets him up. He's still hurting, but he's definitely doing better."

He looked at her and even in the dim light, her face lit up when she smiled. "That's good to hear. Your parents are nice people."

"I never got to properly thank you for all you did the day the accident happened, and for the days that followed. My ma wouldn't have been able to tend to everything on her own."

"She would have," Heather said, sounding as if she were speaking from experience.

Suddenly ashamed, Hayden realized he knew precious little about her background. At first, he'd been consumed with helping his father adjust. Then, after that, he didn't want to seem too interested, afraid she'd get the wrong idea, and he might feel obligated to proceed with the wedding. Humbled, he realized he could have treated Heather a whole lot better. *I will now,* he promised himself.

"Thanks also for recruiting your brother to help me." He glanced away. It was difficult for him to get the words out. "Actually, due to him, I believe we'll make our deadline. He's a darn hard worker."

"Who, Morgan?" She laughed.

He realized she was kidding. "Yes, Morgan. June should be getting back to the livery soon. I'd love to be there when she finds him sleeping in her loft."

"Will she skin him alive?"

"Most likely. She's tough. Doesn't take guff from anyone."

Just then a jackrabbit darted across the road, directly under the horses' hooves. Fritz, the spookier of the pair, jerked his head and surged to the left, dragging Stonewall, the other gelding, along with him and causing the lumber in the back to rattle loudly.

Heather gasped and gripped the seat, startled.

"Easy, Fritz," Hayden crooned. It wasn't long before he had the two animals settled back down to their steady walk.

"That was close!" Heather still had a death grip on the wagon seatback.

"Don't be frightened." He reached over and gently unfurled her fingers from the wooden seat, marveling at how warm and small they felt. He tried to look away, hide how sitting with Heather made him feel. He swallowed.

The vision of all those letters piled in her hands made his stomach tighten. *Who are they from? How had word traveled so fast?*

Could he measure up? Did he want to? "We were never in any real danger." At the split in the road that led to the Holcombs', he reined Fritz and Stonewall left, feeling anything but relieved.

Chapter Nineteen

Evie's face brightened with surprise to find Hayden and Heather standing on her front porch. The dog, who Heather decided must be Dexter, danced around their heels, wagging his tail and whining with excitement.

Because early evening had already descended, Heather missed seeing much of the land, the barns, and the cattle. But that didn't dim her pleasure at seeing her friend in her own home. Imagine that! Little Evie Davenport from St. Louis, wife and owner of a cattle ranch. It was a lot to contemplate. So much had happened in such a short amount of time.

"Your dog's not much of a watchdog, Evie," Hayden teased as they entered the house. He reached down and scratched Dexter behind an ear.

"That's because he knows you, Hayden. He's smart, is all. Why waste his energy barking at you?"

Stopping just inside the door, Heather saw the maple grandfather clock she recognized from the bridal agency. The one Mrs. Seymour had shipped out as a wedding gift. The stately piece looked as if it had been a part of Evie's family for years. Evie had it polished to a sheen, as she always had before.

Hayden shrugged. "You have a point. Chance around? I brought the lumber for your henhouse."

The room smelled of freshly baked bread, and something else. Something sweet. A comfortable-looking yellow settee sat opposite a striking rock fireplace, with a cute little sign that said HOME SWEET HOME. Heather's heart swelled. A taupe-colored chair, one she presumed was Chance's because of the pipe and ashtray on the side table, sat to the left.

"He's in the barn. Go on out. He'll be happy to see you."

Hayden chuckled. "I doubt that. Do you know where he wants me to stack the lumber?"

"Not exactly. It'd be best if you ask him."

"Will do." Hayden made for the door. Before going out he stopped, turned, and looked at Heather, as if to make sure she was all right. A slow smile crept up his face.

The whole scene was surreal. Heather couldn't help but respond with a smile of her own. When he closed the door, Evie rushed to her side.

"What's going on? Have things changed between the two of you?"

Heather took her time looking around. She hated to disappoint Evie. "Not really. I don't know what he's up to. I'm taking each day as it comes."

Heather took Evie's hands in her own. "Give me the grand tour."

"I'd love to." Evie led Heather toward her big stove. "As you can see, the kitchen area is sort of one big room with the living area. Chance made the table and chairs." She winked. "He's so handy."

Heather didn't want to miss a thing. She sensed love everywhere she looked. The beautiful stove Mrs. Seymour had mentioned was the real centerpiece of the home, besides the grandfather clock. A water pump was close by in the sink. Blue flowered curtains hung in the window, and a pie safe graced the wall.

"You've done a wonderful job, Evie. Your home is beautiful."

"I haven't done much. But I do love it here! It's so quiet and peaceful. So different from St. Louis. Once you get used to the sweet-smelling air, nothing else will do."

Evie curled her finger in invitation as she moved toward a door next to the stove. "Come see this." She pushed the door open so Heather could see inside. "Not quite St. Louis, but by next summer I'll have running water inside to make bathing easy. Chance is so thoughtful. It's almost like he just sits around and thinks of ways to make me happy. I can't imagine my life without him."

Evie looked the same on the outside, but Heather could tell she was different. She couldn't put her finger on it—just something warm and confident lighting her from within. Evie was sure of her standing and of her husband's devotion. How intoxicating. With an ache in her heart, Heather realized she wanted it, too. "I'm sure you make him happy right back. I can see it in both your faces."

Emotion welled up inside Heather. She moved on, not wanting to ruin the happy mood. Leaving Evie's soon-to-be-bathroom, she saw another door on the other side of the living area.

"Go ahead. It's the bedroom."

Heather crossed the room, taking everything in. She entered and almost gasped at the sight of the huge bed situated in the middle of a braided rug with its headboard against the wall. Gigantic sawed-off logs were the four posts and a soft-looking quilt covered the rest. It was one of the most spectacular pieces of furniture Heather had ever seen. An oversized window on the opposite wall must give a fantastic view during the day.

"We can see the front pasture from here," Evie said. "All the calves have been born. We only lost one. I adore watching them frolic around while their mamas graze happily throughout the day. Sometimes I stand here a good half hour before I realize what I've done."

"I can't even imagine." Heather glanced at a small book placed on one of the bedposts.

Noticing what her friend was looking at, Evie

picked up the book and held it to her chest. "Last week I started keeping a journal. Years from now, I want to remember everything that's happened. I don't want to forget a thing. Oh—"

Still holding the book, she went to the wardrobe and opened one door. She pulled out a feather duster that Heather recognized immediately. Evie must have brought it all the way from St. Louis, from the days she was the maid at the bride agency. Realization hit Heather. How brave Evie had been, to leave St. Louis on her own and do what she'd done. And look at what she'd gained because of it. Her life. Her destiny.

"I keep this to remind me of where I've come from," Evie said. "To remind me of my mother. To remind me to take chances on things that are important to me." She glanced around the room, a look of wonder on her face, as if seeing her surroundings for the first time. "I can't believe my life has turned out so perfect."

The door opened and the sound of the men's voices filtered into the bedroom. Dexter bounded in through the open door, circling the women with excitement.

Evie laughed. "Sit, Dexter."

He ignored her, ran another quick circle, then pushed his nose into Heather's hand.

"Sit," Evie repeated. She pointed a stern finger into his face. "Sit."

The dog dropped to the floor, placed his muzzle

between his two front paws, and gazed up at Evie with adoring eyes.

Chance appeared in the doorway. "He being a pest? Let me put him out."

"No, leave him." Evie reached down and patted his head.

Heather felt self-conscious being in their bedroom with Chance so close. Behind him, Hayden's gaze caught hers.

Scooting past the men, Heather hurried into the living room.

"The lumber's unloaded," Hayden said, his expression subdued.

His quietness surprised her. Chance hadn't said much either. "We should be getting back. I don't want to keep Heather out too late."

"But you just got here," Evie complained. "I took an apple cake out of the oven ten minutes before you arrived. Stay a little longer and have some."

"Smells good," Hayden admitted.

"It should be cool enough to cut by now. Let me get it from my pie shelf out back." She glanced at the dog as she hurried out the door. "High enough where little paws can't reach."

Evie quickly returned with a square pan, the cake inside a delicate golden brown. She set the dessert on the table, then brought plates with an intricate leaf pattern on the rim from the cupboard. "Please, stay for just a moment—this won't take long. It's been several weeks since we had visitors."

Heather glanced at Hayden and he shrugged. "It's up to you," she said. "You're doing the driving."

"Sure, we'll stay, Evie," Hayden said. "Fritz and Stonewall can practically drive themselves. They know the way back to town even in the dark."

Heather watched Evie slice and serve, marveling at what an accomplished baker she'd become. "It's been a long time since I've had apple cake."

Evie put a fork underneath the first slice and, being careful that the warm cake didn't split in two and fall off her fork, set the piece atop the plate. "It's been tricky learning how to heat my stove like Ina's, so I can bake and not burn everything. But I think I've gotten the hang of it now." Smiling, she passed the plate to Heather. "Go on. Grab yourself a fork and get comfortable. This feels like a tea party."

"This smells wonderful, Evie. I can't wait to try it." Heather went over and sat on one end of the small yellow couch.

Hayden took the plate Evie handed him and headed for the chair. Chance waited for Evie, and then followed her over. He sat on one end of the settee, with Evie in the middle.

Evie fluttered her hand at everyone. "Go on

now, don't be shy." Her color was high, her smile impish.

The reason, Heather was sure, was that she thought Hayden was courting her. She sneaked a look at him. *Is he?* Everything seemed confusing these days.

"This is my very first apple cake, Heather," Evie said. "But don't let that scare you. I'm sure you remember that when I left the bridal agency, I couldn't cook a thing. Well, now I can." She sent Chance a warm, caressing look that had Heather looking away. Evie laughed softly. "Poor Chance. He's so good-natured. And patient, too."

All of a sudden Evie's hand came up to her lips as if she needed to keep the bite she'd just taken from coming out. Her eyes were round and startled. Alarmed, Chance flung his plate into Heather's already-full hands with a clatter as his fork fell to the floor.

He reached out.

"What? What's the matter?"

Evie stood and ran from the room.

Chapter Twenty

When Heather stood to follow Evie, Chance placed a hand on her shoulder, stopping her. "I'll go."

In two strides, he was out of the room, leaving Hayden alone with Heather. It hurt to see the distress on her face. "Don't worry," he said soothingly. "She's probably just excited."

He watched as Heather went around and collected the dishes, taking them to the kitchen sink. She pumped water into a ceramic bowl and quickly washed the four plates and forks. Hayden picked up the dishtowel. "Let me help."

"Thank you." She rinsed the dish then handed it to him.

He'd never felt such anxiety before. Clearly, Evie was Heather's lifeline. He understood that now. Heather found a clean, folded dishtowel in one of the cupboard drawers and covered the cake, tightly tucking the cloth around to prevent it from becoming stale.

"I hope Evie's not upset over something we did," Heather finally said. She must have been thinking about her friend this whole time.

"It couldn't be, Heather. She was having a good time. She's just not feeling well."

The clomp of Chance's boots brought them

around. Evie was by his side, her face a pasty white. "I'm sorry for breaking up the party," she said. "It's been so lovely having you *both* here." She let her gaze linger on him.

Hayden felt a bit self-conscious. He ventured a quick look at Chance, knowing the rancher had never liked him much. Truth was, when the two of them got within spitting distance, they tended to bring out the worst in each other.

Heather stepped forward as if to give her a hug. "No," Evie cautioned, holding her off with her hand. "Don't come too close. I think I may be coming down with something. If either of you gets sick, I'll never forgive myself."

Heather looked at Chance and then over at Evie. "Are you hot? Do you have a fever? I'll ask Dr. Handerhoosen to stop out tomorrow. He won't mind. He just got back from Pine Grove. There've been a few cases of influenza. Maybe it's made its way over here."

Chance pulled Evie tighter to his side. "I'd appreciate that, Heather."

"Chance, I'm as right as rain. There's no need for—"

He hushed her with a look. "I'll be the judge of that."

The moon was beautiful. Prettier than Heather could ever remember. Shimmers of silver and blue painted the quiet land, making her feel tiny in the vast openness. The chilly night air was clean and sweet, something she'd never tire of. The lyrical jingling of Fritz and Stonewall's harness sounded lovely, and the rhythmic clomping of their hooves brought stillness to her soul. When she'd been staying out at the Klinkner's, she'd become quite attached to the gentle beasts.

She darted a glance over at Hayden. "Thank you for the invitation tonight." She could just make out his profile. "I enjoyed visiting with Evie and Chance, even for such a short time. Their home is lovely."

Nodding, he glanced quickly her way, and she thought she caught a smile. "You're welcome. You should plan another trip sometime, during the day. The views of the mountains are spectacular from their homestead. You weren't able to see much in the dark."

She shrugged. Then a giggle slipped out.

She saw him glance over again. "Are you laughing?"

"I guess I was. Just thinking of how much my life has changed since coming to Y Knot. Not in a bad way," she added quickly. "Just different. Now that I'm getting to know a few people, the town is starting to feel like home." *Home.* It was true, but the word still made her heart quiver. *Home is Mother. My brothers and sisters. Home is Melba.*

Hayden flicked the reins and the horses picked up their pace.

"You know, Heather, I really don't know that much about you. Other than you're twenty-two years old, have incredibly beautiful green eyes, come from St. Louis and have a brother who'd like to pound the stuffing out of me, you're a mystery. How about you fill in some of the blanks?"

At his compliment, a warm fuzzy feeling swirled within. *Why is he interested now?* Heather was thankful for the relative darkness. What had brought on this sudden change? Was it the fact that his father was getting better and things at the mill had improved? Or something else? She couldn't guess, but if she were honest with herself, she liked it. "What do you want to know?"

"Let's start with your family. Do you have a large one?"

The faces of her siblings appeared in her mind's eye, bringing a wave of melancholy.

"You could say that. First, there's Travis. He's the oldest at twenty-seven and, since my father's death, he's been the head of the household. He runs the smithy. You've met the second-oldest, Morgan. He's twenty-five. He looks almost identical to Travis, except he's one inch shorter—and a lot funnier. He worked in the smithy too. Well, all of my older brothers work there. Ben is next and just turned twenty-four. Then Peter. He's twenty-three."

A coyote howled from over the ridge. Heather hardly had time to turn toward the sound before the eruption of yipping and screeching got so loud that she jumped.

"Don't be frightened. You want me to light a lantern?"

"No, I'm fine." She pushed away her nerves and pulled her shawl tighter around her shoulders. Y Knot must be getting close. She'd seen one light winking in the distance when they'd topped a ridge. It didn't seem to take this long on the ride out.

"And?" Hayden prompted.

"You sure you want to hear all this? It's pretty boring."

"I asked, didn't I? I think it's interesting."

"Fine. I'm next. The oldest girl. After me are two more brothers, Curtis at twenty and Sam at nineteen."

Hayden let go a long whistle. "That's some family. I'm jealous."

Was he being serious? He had a beautiful home, a profitable business. Her family just eked by each year putting food on the table and clothes on everyone's backs.

"Are you making fun of me?"

His head jerked around and he looked at her for several moments. "I'm not being sarcastic. I'm serious. I think a home full to bursting is great. Being an only child got lonely. I'd like to have a large family someday."

She'd not let him know how much his comment pleased her. She'd always wanted a large family, too. Just like the one she grew up in.

"Please go on." His request was so contrite and heartfelt she couldn't deny him.

"Fine. There are three more. All girls. Sally, eighteen; Anita, sixteen; and the baby, Melba, is fourteen."

She tried to mask the sorrow in her voice when she said Melba's name, but perhaps she hadn't succeeded because he pulled the horses down to a slow walk and then a halt. She felt conspicuous just sitting there as he continued looking at her. What the heck did he want?

"Melba sounds special to you."

"She is."

"Why?" He asked the question so softly it was almost lost in the coyote song.

Now he was getting personal. Too personal. She didn't owe him any answers, especially one like that. She'd share her family with him, but she sure wasn't going to share her heart.

She heard him shift in his seat. "Sorry. I shouldn't have asked. That's none of my business."

Hoofbeats sounded coming up the road. The moon had slipped behind some low-hanging clouds, making the night quite dark. Who would be out riding now? When Hayden reached down, pulled a holster from under the wagon seat, and slipped the gun out, fear swirled within.

Chapter Twenty-One

"Don't worry," Hayden said, leaning over so he could keep his voice low. "This is just for insurance. It's most likely someone I know."

The rider stopped a good distance away. He'd seen them, too.

Hayden waited. The rider called out, "Hello in the wagon."

Hayden relaxed and set the gun on the seat between them. "It's Roady Guthrie."

Heather let go a breath.

Roady approached in the darkness of the night. When he was a few feet away, Hayden could make out some resemblance to the cowboy, and the distinct outline of Roady's mount.

"Hayden," he said. He touched his hat. "Miss Stanford."

"Mr. Guthrie."

"Nice weather for a *Tuesday* night ride?"

His tone was neither mocking nor challenging, yet Hayden knew it was ripe with meaning. The McCutcheon ranch hand was irritated he'd stolen her away before Roady had the chance to call on her Thursday night.

"I had lumber to deliver out to the Holcombs'. Thought Heather might like to ride along. We had many conversations about her friendship with Evie when she was living at my house."

Roady chuckled. "I'm sure you did. Four whole days there. You must have had a heck of a lot of free time on your hands."

"Four and a half."

Roady chuckled again, a little louder. "Did he show you the agate outcropping along the creek?" he asked Heather. "It's real pretty. Perfect place for a picnic."

"No, he didn't."

"Shame on you, Hayden," Roady scolded. "The agate would've been the first thing I'd show her if I was taking a beautiful woman out to the Holcombs'."

"Too dark by the time we got close to the ranch," Hayden replied. "I didn't want her to twist an ankle."

"Understandable. Well, we'll go there first, Miss Stanford—while it's still light—on Thursday evening. Bring along some comfortable walking boots. It's a little way off the road."

"I will, Mr. Guthrie," she answered. "Being from the city, I love venturing out into the land. Thank you for thinking of it. And if you'd like, you may call me Heather."

"My pleasure . . . Heather. Well, I better get back to the ranch if I want any grub left. You have a nice time. Good night, *Heather*. I'll see you *Thursday* afternoon."

"Good night, Mr. Guthrie. I'll be ready."

Roady loped off.

Hayden gritted his teeth, then flicked the reins over the horses' backs. It shouldn't matter a whit to him who she stepped out with. Hell, all those letters back at the boardinghouse should give her plenty of opportunities.

Rounding onto Main Street, they passed the Biscuit Barrel, dark and buttoned up for the night. He pulled the wagon to a halt at the boardinghouse. Lights glowed from all the upstairs rooms except on the far left. That must be Heather's.

"Here we are," Hayden said. They hadn't said much since running into that skunk, Roady. What was he up to? He didn't own a house. He'd never said he had a burning desire to settle down. Have a *passel* of *young'uns*. Hayden smirked to himself. *I guess the right girl had a way of changing a man's mind about things like that.*

He got out and walked around the back of the wagon and up to Heather's side. That's when he noticed the musician and another man sitting in the rocking chairs, talking.

Without a word, he reached up and she took his hand, her fingers small and warm within his own. His body reacted. He longed to pull her close. Kiss her lips. Tell her how pretty she looked in the soft light of the moon.

Wait, this isn't making any sense.

When had he started thinking of moonlight?

Heck—about proposing to the loveliest girl in the world?

On the porch, he opened the door, ignoring the others. Inside, a lantern burned on the supper table as well as on a side table by the stairs. The aroma of whatever they'd eaten for dinner hung heavy in the air. *She hasn't eaten!*

"Heather, I just realized you didn't get any supper. I'm sorry. How stupid can I be? That little bit of apple cake wasn't enough to feed a mouse. Are you famished?"

"I'm a little hungry. But you didn't eat either. You must be starved yourself."

Embarrassment engulfed him. "Actually, I did eat before stopping here. Ma was fixing supper for Pa and heated me up a plate of leftovers from last night. And Evie's apple cake helped."

"Should we go into the kitchen and see what I can find? I have a talent for making something out of nothing, at least that's what my brothers and sisters tell me. If I don't, I may not be able to get to sleep." She patted her tummy.

He nodded, following her into the kitchen and quietly closed the door. She struck a match and lit a lantern on the sideboard. Being in here with her felt right, as if they were bonded together. The room was quiet and warm. There was barely enough light to see. He pulled up a chair as she went into the pantry and came back with a loaf of bread. She set it on the drainboard.

"I'm sorry. I spoke too soon. Lou's pantry is pretty well picked clean. I can remember a few days back in St. Louis when I was growing up when the cupboards were just as bare."

This was new. She was opening up. He was afraid to comment for fear she'd stop.

Taking a knife, she sliced off a piece and handed it to him. He pulled around another chair and she sat down. They ate in silence.

"My mama used to make bone soup sometimes when there was nothing to eat," she said after she finished her last bite. She dusted the crumbs from her hands. "I was little and can hardly remember. Not with a stone, like the folk tale, but a single bone, if she had one."

"I remember the story."

"I didn't even know there was a fable about stone soup until our Portuguese gardener at the bride agency told it one day. Anyway, my mother would say, 'Look at this delicious bone! Let's get it cooking so there's something for your father and brothers when they get home from work.' Travis and Morgan were both working in the smithy by then, carrying things and mucking out stalls. Travis couldn't have been more than nine and had been working for two years." Heather cut another hunk of bread for him, and another for herself. "I'll replace this in the morning. Lou assured me I was welcome to raid the pantry if I got hungry."

He took a bite and chewed, unable to tear his gaze away.

"My mother, with those green eyes I remember so well, was beautiful. She would hold that bone so reverently—as if it were a three-pound roast. 'Now, Sissy,'—that's what she called me because I was the only girl at that time—'Let's wash this bone and put it in a pot to boil. You'll see, it'll be delicious.' Benjamin and Peter, older than me but not old enough to go to work, would watch suspiciously, whispering behind their hands. But I always believed." Heather laughed and shook her head. "My stomach would growl and she'd pat my head. 'Soon, Sissy, soon supper will be ready.' "

Hayden was spellbound. He could tell she wasn't just sharing, but reliving her past. He ached to hold her. Take her home and cook her supper with all the fixings. Drive the hurtful memories away and create happy ones of their own. Memories to last a lifetime.

"Well, what happened? Did the bone turn into supper?"

She tipped her head and her eyebrow rose. This was definitely a side he'd never seen.

"What do you think? Are you a believer?"

No, he wasn't, actually. He believed in God, in his country, in his family. He believed that hard work paid off. He believed people could change—yes, he absolutely believed that because he'd been doing his share of changing ever since Heather had arrived in Y Knot. But he didn't believe in magic.

"Hayden?"

Darn. He didn't want this to end. If he said no—

"You're not. I can see it in your eyes. That's all right. As my mother used to tell me, there are enough believers in the world to make up for Doubting Thomases."

Chapter Twenty-Two

Morgan was almost asleep, stretched out on his blanket in the hayloft of June Pittman's livery, when the livery door below opened and the sound of someone walking around brought him fully awake.

"How you doing, Salty?" The hinge on Salty's stall door squeaked loudly when whoever was down there opened it. The sound of the horse blowing dust from his nostrils was loud in the quiet barn. "Hush. You'll wake all the others."

All the others? Was she—it was a female by the sound of her voice—calling the horses "others"? Being considerate not to wake them? Or was she talking about the motley flock of chickens that pooped everywhere he wanted to step and refused to go into their coop?

He heard another sound. *What was that? A kiss?* Was she kissing the horse? Morgan rolled his lips over his teeth to keep from laughing. He edged up on his elbow so he could hear better. She was still in Salty's stall. Kissing her horse. Yes. That's exactly what it was. He rocked with silent laughter until tears escaped his eyes. Oh, this was good. He wiped the moisture with the back of his arm.

"I'll be right back." Now she was—was—

coming up the loft ladder! "I'll get you a little midnight snack."

Panicked, Morgan sat up, groping in the darkness for his shirt. Where had he put the darn thing? She was at the top of the ladder, now stepping onto the loft floor.

She pulled up. Must have felt his presence. If he said anything now to announce his presence, she might spook—causing her to fall and break her neck. She stood like a statue, her raspy breathing now loud in his ears.

Only one thing to do. He lunged up, caught her belt, and pulled her forward, away from the edge.

Surprised, she came up fighting.

"Hold on!" Morgan shouted.

She wasn't holding. She swung and connected with his jaw. And damn, she packed a wallop.

Morgan rolled back on his heel but she launched herself at him like a panther, knocking him backward. Wanting nothing more than to rub his stinging jaw, he boomed, "Stop it! I'm not—"

They rolled as he tried to pin her arms, coming dangerously close to the drop. Hell, he didn't feel like falling to the hard-packed floor. He might have to knock some sense into this crazy woman.

In one swift move, she slipped out from under his arm, zipped around and wrapped her arm around his neck, locking it with her other one. His hands came up and grasped her forearm.

He yanked, trying to get some air. Her muscle bulged. No wonder she was getting the best of him. This woman was a stud!

Morgan's temper flared. His patience hit an end. He leaned back slightly, a move he'd perfected with his brother Travis, and without missing a beat, gripped her arm at his neck and flung all his weight forward.

She flipped over his head onto the straw, landing on her back.

He pounced, pinning her down with his weight, and wrestled first one arm and then the other above her head, placing both her wrists into one of his hands. With the other, he wiped at blood that was oozing from his bottom lip.

"Are you crazy?" he said through clenched teeth. "Settle down. I'm not going to hurt you."

"Let me up!" She bucked. Even in the dark interior of the barn, he could see her eyes alive with anger—and a little fear.

He didn't want to scare her, but he didn't want another punch in the face, either. "I'll do no such thing. You gave me a bloody lip. And I think you loosened one of my teeth."

Her gaze darted around as if searching for a weapon. "What are you doing in my barn? Hiding out?"

She was calming down. Her voice held a semblance of sanity.

"Get off me, you brute!"

Well, maybe not. "And risk another punch in the face? Not on your life!"

"Who are you? I've never seen you before. Why are you hiding out in my livery? Are you an outlaw?"

He chuckled.

She glowered.

"You're just full of questions, aren't you?"

"You're dang right, I am. I come home to some bum hanging out on my property. I'll get the sheriff. Have you arrested."

She'd stopped fighting him and now lay quiet on her back, with her hands pinned above her head under his hand. Small beads of sweat trickled off her temple and into her hair. Her nostrils flared with each breath she took as she struggled to get air. Was it safe to let her up? Actually, he felt a twinge of embarrassment when he realized just how small she really was. "Are you June Pittman?"

"Of *course* I'm June Pittman. Who else did you think?"

Morgan rubbed his jaw, then slipped sideways and rolled to his knees. He extended his hand to help her.

She waved him off and stood quickly, brushing off the straw and hay that clung in her hair and on her clothes. Then she nailed him with a frosty gaze. "Now that you know who I am, who the heck are you?"

"You don't know me."

"I know. That's why I asked."

"It's a long story."

"Start at the beginning."

Suddenly conscious of his semidressed state, Morgan looked around for his shirt. Spying the garment hanging from a nail, he nonchalantly slipped it on.

"Well?" she said impatiently. "I'm waiting. Are you going to tell me who you are or should I go wake up Jack Jones and have him arrest you for trespassing?"

The last thing Morgan needed was to get in trouble with the law. "No, don't do that. My name is Morgan Stanford. I've been in town less than a week."

"Staying here the whole time?"

He nodded.

She crossed her arms over her chest, waiting for him to go on.

"Heather Stanford is my sister."

Her eyebrow cocked up. "And—who is Heather?"

"She was the mail-order bride Hayden Klinkner sent for . . . well actually, his mother sent for."

June's mouth gaped and her arms dropped to her sides. All agitation left her face. "Hayden!" She burst into laughter. "What's all this about? I haven't heard a thing about it."

"Well, you will. As soon as you're back in town

for all of one minute. Seems that's all anyone is talking about. The Mail-Order Bride Done Wrong."

"So, why are you here? Do you come with the deal? Mail-order brother-in-law?"

"Very funny." He gestured to the loft ladder. "I'd feel more comfortable taking this conversation downstairs, out of my bedroom, with *the others*."

June nodded, missing his innuendo.

He stood back as she went to the loft edge.

She was already on the third rung of the ladder when she glanced up at him, the smile on her lips telling him she wasn't going to summon the deputy after all.

Chapter Twenty-Three

In her room, Heather looked at the stack of letters on top of the tall chest of drawers where she'd left them earlier. Her stomach churned. Her distress was partly from regret that her life had turned into a sideshow for all to see, and partly from knowing that even if there were a letter from the prince of Peru, no one would ever take the place of Hayden Klinkner.

Taking the mail and the cup of tea she prepared after Hayden had left, Heather ventured to the small chintz chair in the corner of her bedroom and set her cup on the round accent table, careful not to spill any of the hot liquid. Sitting, she lit her second lantern, then gazed at the posts on her lap.

Flipping through, she found she had no desire to open any of them. Why should she? Some of the printing was neat, some messy with phonetically spelled words. At least the bachelors were showing gumption. Midway through the stack, she paused to sip her cooling tea. Here was one all the way from Waterloo! She must be the talk of the territory. The thought did not bring her happiness.

She began flipping through the letters again and almost spilled her tea. A letter from Sally!

Happiness coursed through her. And—a letter from Lina! Setting her tea and the rest of the letters aside, Heather opened the post from her fanciful little sister who loved to write. Four pages were stuffed inside the envelope.

    Sissy, how are you? We all were excited to get your letter, but also sad hearing what happened to your soon-to-be father-in-law. By now, God willing, he should be feeling a little better—and perhaps the wedding plans have already gone forward. I remember when Morgan's horse fell on him and broke his leg in two places. That was horrible and something I try not to think about. I am sorry you have to experience such difficulties at a time that should be the happiest in your life. When I read that part aloud to Mother, she promptly said her favorite line—I am sure you know what I am about to say—Everything happens for a reason, we just do not know what that reason is yet.
    Everything sounds so nice in your new town. Your in-laws' home sounds wonderfully beautiful. I cannot imagine such a bedroom as the one you described. I would feel like a princess sleeping there and never leave the feather mattress or the down coverlet. Things have turned

out so glorious for you, I am thinking of applying at the mail-order bride agency myself. I would love to have an adventure of my own—especially with a man as charming and handsome as your Hayden. And when you write of the fresh, clean air, the pretty river that flows in the back of the mill, of the mountains filled with trees, deer, birds of all kinds, I want to fly to you straight away. Mother insists I am much too young at eighteen, and that I should wait until I am at least twenty or twenty-two but I think that is too old! What is your opinion? (Not saying you are old!)

Heather paused, a smile cheering her heart. Old? She felt so young. Inexperienced. With a shaky hand, she took a sip of her tea and continued.

Or, if I decide not to marry, maybe the town you live in needs a journalist. You know how I love to write, and my spelling is impeccable, so besides being a wife and mother, I think I could be happy being a writer. Just yesterday, I submitted a small piece to the paper on the quilts Aunt Tillie and Mother and their small group were making for the families that suffered in the fire last year. Mr. Greenstein might run my story in next week's society page. Imagine that!

But enough about me. The big news as of yesterday is that Travis and Peggy Lee are off. No one knows the reason. However, I am working on that. Aunt Tillie has yet to deliver and we are waiting impatiently for the new arrival.

I know you are waiting for news of Melba, but I saved that for last because it is not good. Mother sits at her side, day and night, expecting the worst. My heart is breaking for both of them. Mother has aged ten years in the last week as the doctors have told us there is nothing to be done. They advised us to spend time with her and tell her all the things we will want to before she leaves us for good. I still cannot believe that is going to happen. She is cheerful, the happy little angel she always is, and says she is going to be with Papa soon. She told me to put in this letter for you NOT to be sad. That she is not in pain. That she is not afraid to die and is actually looking forward to heaven and seeing the face of God. Sissy, it breaks my heart. She is only fourteen and yet is so much more mature than either Anita or me.

I have to go now because I want to be able to post this letter today, and if I do not sign off I will miss my chance. I love you. And miss you. But I am so excited for you, too. Know you own all our hearts, and you are never far from our thoughts.
All my love,
Sally
Post Script: Please give all my love to my new and only brother-in-law!

With a shaky hand, Heather wiped away the tears that had spilled over. Her breath shuddered. She missed home. And her sweet Sally. And of course, Melba. *Everyone.*

Her biggest regret was that she'd never see Melba in this world again. She remembered her last day at home, when she'd said her good-byes. Melba had been so brave, the only one not crying. Pledging her heart forever, she told Heather to go to Montana, live a good, event-filled life, something she herself could not do. She would wait for news . . . happy, joyful letters chock-full of what the West was like, the sight of her first real Indian, what it was like to stand under the expansive blue sky, being the only person as far as the eye could see. She'd wait for letters like those to pass the time.

No matter how tired she was, Heather always added some paragraphs to the letter she sent off every few days. Giving Melba pleasure through writing stories of life in the West helped ease some of the pain of being away from her dear little sister at the close of her life.

Heather closed her eyes and rubbed them sadly. Though the hour grew late and five in the morning would come all too soon, she reached for Lina's letter. Even if she went to bed now, there wasn't a chance she'd fall asleep. Besides, she was awash with curiosity how things had turned out for her dearest friend. She needed something else to think about to get her thoughts off Melba.

Heather sipped her now tepid tea, and glanced at the clock on the dresser. It was almost midnight.

Dear Heather,

I was so grateful to receive your letter, although I'm so curious to hear about your meeting with Mr. Klinkner. I want to know what you think of him and every detail of your wedding. So don't keep me waiting for long!

As for me, I'm preparing to set out for Sweetwater Springs. When next you write, send the letter there.

Each day I return from visiting my family with more to take with me on my journey—mostly food. My relatives are so afraid I won't be able to make Italian meals for my family, so they're sending me off with dried herbs, pasta, dried tomatoes, and garlic. I'm so glad Mrs. Hensley gave me one of her old trunks. Otherwise, I couldn't possibly transport everything!

Today, Tio Guido handed me two bottles of Chianti, and Tia Maria pressed a big block of Parmesan cheese into my arms. I'm afraid that feather bed Mrs. Hensley gave me will smell like food, which might not be bad for me—a reminder of home. But I doubt Mr. Barrett will want to sleep in a bed that smells like garlic, cheese, and spices!

Love,
Lina

Delightful! Lina had raised her spirits without even trying. Imagining her friend arriving in Sweetwater Springs with all that good food made a small giggle escape Heather's lips. Lina was going to fatten Jonah up, whether he wanted it or not. Heather had gone with her once to visit Lina's family for dinner, and had watched in wonder as the group at the dinner table all talked without listening—everyone at once. She'd wondered how anyone understood each other, yet they did. The love that abided in those walls was a beautiful thing.

Heather's eyelids finally began to droop. Was Hayden home? Had he already dressed in his bedclothes and retired? Was he snuggled in his bed? She'd never seen inside his small home behind his parents' place, but that hadn't stopped her from wondering what his house was like.

She glanced down at her own state of dress and knew she needed to get up and prepare for bed, but her legs wouldn't comply. She yawned, then listened to the quiet, thinking she didn't have the energy to get out of her dress, petticoat, and corset. Tonight, the wagon ride with Hayden had been wonderful and heartbreaking at the same time. Roady Guthrie was a mystery, too. These Western men. Who knew what made them tick?

Chapter Twenty-Four

"Up here, Morgan," Hayden shouted, waving his arm to get Morgan's attention. When Heather's brother looked up, Hayden pointed to the left, where Morgan needed to adjust the log on the mill carriage. With the steam engine up and running, he and Morgan were making up for lost time. "Hold the log steady and I'll be right there."

Hayden shoved the saw handle in the off position and strode to the back of the milling shed, where Morgan had reattached the same oversized log three times. They'd hand cut it before bringing it in, but the milling would still take the better part of the day to get it through the process, resulting in a stack of lumber. If they kept going at this pace, as backbreaking as the work was, they would fulfill the Night Owl contract with one day to spare.

When Hayden approached, Morgan stepped back, giving him room. "Try cinching the belt tighter in the beginning." With the log in position, Hayden clapped Morgan on the shoulder. "How about a break? I know I can use one."

Morgan nodded. "Sure. Sounds good."

They both took their bandannas from around their necks and swabbed the sweat from their faces. A bluish tint shadowed one of Morgan's eyes. He'd told Hayden about how he'd met June in the loft, then had gone quiet on the subject ever since. A man had a right to his privacy, so Hayden had given him plenty of space.

"Thirsty?" Hayden asked.

"Always."

They headed behind the shed. Years ago, Hayden's father had diverted part of the river to bring a fast-flowing stream down from the hillside. They kept a bucket there for drinking. Hayden dipped the wooden container in and handed it to Morgan, who drank then poured the remainder over his head. Hayden took the bucket and did the same.

They stood in companionable silence for a few minutes.

Morgan rubbed his hand over his face. "I saw Heather this morning on her way to Dr. Handerhoosen's office. Her eyes were red. She'd been crying."

A whisper of sadness squeezed Hayden's heart. Crying? Averting his face, he watched as an eagle hung on the wind above the river. Yeah, well, he'd lain awake until he'd heard the roosters crowing. Some mess his mother had created, but he was perpetuating the problem himself by thinking about her all the time and taking her on moonlight rides. "Did she say why?"

"No. I didn't ask. She did say the two of you took a ride out to see her friend." The tone of

Morgan's voice made Hayden turn and look him in the face.

"You have something to say?"

"Just that Heather's been through enough already. She doesn't need you stomping all over her heart while you try to figure out what you want. She's taking the brunt of your indecision. There are more than enough upstanding men who're interested in her. Ones who would make her a fine husband. Don't mess that up for her."

Morgan was right. He was making this harder for Heather. He should never have stopped by yesterday. He'd known the outing was a mistake, and yet . . . he hadn't been able to stop himself. And the time out to the Holcombs' and back were the happiest moments he'd had since she'd left his parents' house.

"Hayden?"

"I hear you, Morgan. I understand."

"Good. Just wanted to make sure you knew I won't stand for you hurting her twice. As long as we're in agreement there, everything else is good."

"Everything is good then." *Liar!*

"Hayden! Morgan!" Ina called from the house.

"Back here," he shouted, striding around the building. He stopped on the mill side of the road. His father sat in a chair on the porch and his mother was wiping her hands on a dishcloth just inside the door. He loved them, yes, he did. But what else did he want? Was this the extent of his life? Alone?

His mother smiled and waved. "I've just taken an apple pie out of the oven. You and Morgan come in in about half an hour. It should be cool by then."

He nodded. "Thanks, Ma," he shouted back. "We will."

A vision of Heather, as she'd been the day Francis stopped by asking for lumber for Luke, came to him. He embellished the dream, imagining Heather with a babe in her arms and another hanging on her skirt.

Blinking, he noticed his father looking at him. When Hayden smiled, his pa nodded. "Looking good, son. Sorry I've left this all to you. It's a heck of a lot of work."

"No problem, Pa," he answered, feeling Morgan's presence now at his side. "You'll be up and back to work in no time. Just rest."

"I am, thanks to you and Morgan."

"They're good people," Morgan said quietly.

Hayden turned and headed back toward the milling shed. "I'm amazed that you can say that, considering."

Dr. Handerhoosen placed his palm on Heather's forehead. "You feeling all right? Your eyes are red and your smile has gone missing. How does your throat feel?"

Heather leaned on the long handle of the broom, propping herself up. She was exhausted, having lain awake all night. Morgan had noticed her red eyes and now it seemed Dr. Handerhoosen had, too.

"Fine. I'm just a bit worn out."

"Well, don't get worn too thin. Like I said yesterday, several cases of influenza have broken out in Pine Grove. Working too hard can weaken your constitution, making you susceptible. I'm cutting your hours back so you don't have to get up so early."

She smiled, knowing he'd do no such thing. They'd already had this conversation a couple of times. Dr. Handerhoosen was like a big cuddly bear. She liked him and wished she could do more to be of help. "I'll get up early anyway, Doctor. I enjoy my mornings here."

"I know you do. And I sure do appreciate them. Since Dr. Nord's practice never materialized as we'd expected, and Y Knot keeps growing, I stay pretty busy. I think after a week, though, the early rising and all your chores are taking their toll. Wouldn't want you to get sick."

"I come from a family of ten children, Dr. Handerhoosen, and have been exposed to just about everything there is. I was just feeling a little homesick last night. But since you brought the subject up, I'd like to do more to assist you. Doctoring, that is."

He gazed thoughtfully out the window for a minute, then turned and looked at her. "I'll certainly give that some thought. It's not a bad idea at all. You were very good helping with Norman." He winked. "Still, I want you to know if there's anything you need or want to talk about, I'm always here with an open ear. It must be difficult for you to be away from home and then have the rug pulled out from under your feet."

Feeling self-conscious, she took the broom and reached under the examination table for a nonexistent dust ball and made sweeping motions toward the door, just for something to do. In two days, she'd gotten the place shipshape. Now, keeping the two rooms that way was easy. She'd carefully emptied all the jars of their contents, washed and dried the glass until each sparkled, and replaced everything. She'd washed his curtains, then took them back to the boardinghouse and ironed them.

"Thank you for your concern, but I'm fine. Really."

"If you say so. But if this ever gets to be too much, and you want to quit, I won't hold it against you. Now, hand over that broom. It's time for you to skedaddle over to Berta May's. At least her building has better ventilation and is a bit cooler than this place." He swabbed his moist forehead. "I'll see you tomorrow."

As Heather strolled down the boardwalk toward

the sewing shop, she wondered how Morgan was doing with Hayden out at the mill. Were they getting the lumber cut fast enough to fill the order? She hadn't shared Sally's news about Melba with her brother this morning because she didn't want to put a damper on his day.

"Morning, Miss Stanford," a tall, good-looking young man said nervously. He'd come out of the leather shop just as she approached. His clothes—overalls and work boots—were more farmer than cowboy. She had no idea who he was.

"Good day," she responded as she walked past. She didn't want to be impolite, but she had no desire to get involved in a conversation with a man who might be interested in courting her. She zeroed in on her destination ahead, hoping he'd get the hint, and continued walking. Fast.

His boot steps quickly approached her from behind.

"Excuse me, miss."

She stopped and turned.

He caught up with her in one stride. Whipping the hat from his head, he held the battered, sweat-stained thing to his chest. He looked terribly shy and rather handsome at the same time. "Yes?"

"I'm new to town, miss, but I know by your description that you're Miss Heather Stanford, that Mail-Order Bride Done—"

He clapped his mouth closed and his face turned red.

What am I supposed to say to that?

"What I meant to say, is you're the girl from St. Louis that's looking for a husband. I was wondering if I might stop by the boardinghouse sometime soon, sit out on the porch and talk a spell. I saw some nice big rockers. Just so we might get to know each other a little."

As she gazed into the young man's earnest face, her mind went blank. She was exhausted, hungry—not having eaten this morning for lack of appetite—and her heart ached thinking of her lovely wagon ride with Hayden out to Evie's.

"Can't you see she's just being polite, farm boy! Go on and let her be. Go write yourself a letter and send it. She's not taking anyone out of line."

Chapter Twenty-Five

Shocked at the forceful speech, Heather spun around to see who was talking. A pint-sized woman stood on the boardwalk, hands on hips, wearing men's pants and shirt. A brown ponytail stuck out from under a black cowboy hat. She looked more boy than girl.

"Go on!" the woman commanded, taking a step toward the man. She gave him a squinty-eyed look until he took a stumbling step back. "If you want to meet her so badly, go on and write her a letter like the rest of the fellers. There's a stack of posts in Lichtenstein's a foot tall. She'll get it."

His Adam's apple bobbed. "But I came all this—" He caught her look. "All right, I will." He cast Heather's champion a disparaging look, then blurted, "I'll write that letter, Miss Heather. My name is Tobit Preece! Be watching for it! I want to marry you."

He turned and disappeared into the crowd of men that had gathered behind him.

"Didn't you hear me?" June said, waving her arm at the group. "All you men leave Miss Stanford alone. If you're interested in her, send her a note. If you can't write, have someone write it for you. Don't be pestering her on the street! That's not nice. And if you don't abide what I just said, well, I'll come teach you some manners."

The woman drew herself up and Heather would have sworn she grew a good three inches. Reminded her a bit of her brothers, if that were possible. It was obvious these men knew her and took her threat seriously.

The crowd dispersed. Relieved, Heather exhaled a deep breath. "Thank you. I appreciate your coming to my rescue. I'm Heather."

"You're welcome."

A few people walked by, giving the two women a wide berth.

"Who are you, if you don't mind my asking?"

"Name's June Pittman. I own the livery and smithy in town."

Heather couldn't contain her smile. "June! I'm so happy to meet you. I feel as if I know you already from all the things Hayden and Chance have said about you."

"All disparaging, I'm sure."

"Not at all—why would you say that? All good things. I've been in your livery. I like it—especially your chickens."

June flashed a warning look at a rider that was coming too close with an envelope in his hand.

"How did you know who I was?" Heather continued. "I hope you don't mind, but Jack gave us permission for my brother, Morgan, to use your forge. He needed to make some parts for Hayden's steam engine for the mill, seeing as how you were gone and couldn't do it. Did you just get back today?"

June held up her hand. "Just slow down. I can only answer one question at a time." She was stern and businesslike but Heather could tell that June liked her. She was all bluster and no bite.

"Have you met Morgan yet? He's been sleeping in your livery."

Now she looked a little cranky.

"I did. Last night around eleven. About scared the life out of me and then about beat the stuffing from my hide."

Heather pulled back. She didn't believe a word of it. "No. He wouldn't do that."

June pointed to an abrasion on her forehead. "You sure?"

"Well, not on purpose."

"Who said anything about on purpose?"

Heather laughed. "Come on. Walk with me over to Berta May's. No one in this town would dare bother me with you at my side."

With a wide grin, June nodded and fell into step.

"So, I gather your meeting with Morgan didn't go well?"

June laughed. "Let's just say he startlcd mc, then I beat the stuffing outta him."

They were in front of Berta May's shop. Several men watched from a safe distance. "You're a rare commodity, you know that, Miss

Stanford? Men outnumber women fifty to one out here in Montana. I heard about your misfortune with Hayden, but I'm not surprised. And in any event, there will be a lot of men wanting to take his place."

Right now Heather didn't want to contemplate anyone else. Her heart needed a rest. *She* needed a rest. Working, eating, and sleeping sounded fine to her. Just existing and not thinking about the future.

Berta May came to the door to greet her. "Good morning, Heather. June. Good to see you back in town."

"Yeah, I'm glad to be back. Seems Y Knot has had lots of excitement while I was away."

She gestured to Heather and a warm sentiment ran through Heather's heart. She liked June Pittman. She certainly felt safe around her. They would be friends. What was better than that?

Berta May was always dressed to the hilt, even while at work. Her fancy turnout was especially unusual in such a remote town. She had confided to Heather that she'd never given up hope that someday she'd marry. The flurry with all the bachelors walking by her shop had her smiling broadly as she tried to catch some of the attention. Today she wore a tight-fitting blue calico dress with a bustle and bow. She also sported a fetching little pillbox hat and boots so shiny they'd spook a dead-broke horse. Though she was already in her midforties, no one dared utter the term *old maid* around her.

"Do you have some work for me, Berta May?" Heather asked.

"Yes, I do. A winter coat that needs letting out. All the seams, sleeves, and hem. Mr. Beaverton has put on some weight since last year and wants it to be ready for this winter. I saved the project for you."

Heather nodded, happy to have work no matter what it was.

"Sounds like drudgery to me," June said under her breath. "I'd rather muck ten stalls than sit hunched over a coat, ripping out the—"

Berta May rolled her eyes. "We get your point, June. To each his or her own."

June nodded. "Guess you're right. Well, I'll leave you two to your drudg—er, work." Before Heather even had a chance to say good-bye, the spunky little blacksmith was gone.

After a light noontime meal at the boardinghouse, Heather started for Lichtenstein's Provisions with barely any energy to spare. She'd gotten over half the seams ripped out of Mr. Beaverton's winter coat and would finish the grueling task tomorrow. The heavy garment was constructed out of a tough canvas material and her fingers were sore. The tip of her right index finger had started bleeding and that's when Berta May told her to finish the project tomorrow. Everyone, it seemed, was afraid of working her too hard.

Heather pulled the door open into Lichtenstein's and stepped into the cool interior. As usual, the store was quiet.

"I'm here, Mr. Simpson." She looked around, then smiled at the clerk when she spotted him by the potato barrel. "What would you like me to do? The books won't take me but a few minutes."

Once she got used to the alphabetical way Mr. Lichtenstein liked his items displayed, she found the system quite refreshing. She'd never seen a store organized that way before.

The old man reached under the counter. "Here," he growled. "You can take these off my hands." With a clunk, he set a stack of mail on the counter. "All for you. Yesterday was just a warm-up for today. There are twenty-two in all for the Mail-Order Bride of Y Knot, Montana. That's you, missy."

Heather couldn't believe what she was seeing. "No." She approached slowly and eyed the stack, a sick feeling turning her stomach sour. "But I don't want them. I never asked for this. What can I do to make it stop?"

"Only one thing. Get hitched. And soon!" He pushed the stack of mail toward her, then turned and stomped to the back room, grumbling all the way.

Chapter Twenty-Six

Hayden and Morgan exchanged glances as they stepped through the saloon doors. The lengthy wooden bar was crowded, with not a place to squeeze in. "I say we have an auction among the top five men she approves!" an unknown man shouted above the din in the saloon. "Kind of hurry her along a bit. She came out here to wed a husband and a husband she will have." He took his hat off and waved it grandly about. "There's two dozen men here happy to oblige. She's had plenty long enough to make up her mind."

The men clustered about murmured their approval, each most likely thinking he'd be one of the approved five.

Hayden made for the near end of the bar by the window, where he'd spotted practically the only space in the establishment yet unspoken for. Morgan followed. A mixture of emotions rolled around inside him. Anger at these stupid men, uncertainty for Heather's future.

"She's only been here a week, Martin!" another fellow replied. "Give her more time." He was relatively clean and his clothes looked washed and pressed, a stark contrast to the man who'd thrown out the audacious suggestion for hurrying Heather along in her decision making.

"A week here in Y Knot proper, maybe. Don't forget she spent three or four days out at Klinkner's Mill."

"You can't auction off a woman these days! It ain't legal." The portly man pounded his empty glass on the bar, sloshing the contents everywhere. "What I wanna know is, has she started reading the letters yet? She won't say boo to any of us if we see her on the street. It's getting a mite irritating."

The last comment bolstered Hayden's spirits. *Maybe she isn't set on marrying just anyone.*

Everywhere Hayden looked ranchers, businessmen, and cowboys—some he knew and many he'd never seen before—talked in agitated excitement. Some were gussied up, others looked as if they needed a trip to the bathhouse and barber. Because of the latter group, a rancid mixture of sweat, whiskey, and sour manure, much stronger than normal, hung in the air.

Fancy flitted here and there, her cork-lined wooden tray poised on one hand and held high in the air. Shot glasses and beer mugs tottered and tipped, but somehow none spilled. Her high-heeled boots tapped out a tempo as she hurried back and forth. This boring little cow town had just come to life.

"What do you make of it?" Hayden asked Morgan quietly, leaning forward onto his forearms.

Morgan's eyes glittered dangerously. "Don't like it."

"Me either. Trouble's brewing. One or two of these blowhards are going to get tired of waiting, feel entitled. Heather doesn't know the stir she's creating."

Hayden wondered if he dared ask the question that had been on his mind for days. He and Morgan had found equal footing. Maybe he wouldn't mind. "Morgan, can I ask you a question?"

Morgan turned and looked at him. "Shoot."

"What made Heather want to be a mail-order bride? I don't get it. She's beautiful. And sweet to talk to. And, heck, she even cooks well. I'd think she'd be able to marry just about anyone she wanted. Why take a chance on an unknown?"

Morgan drummed his fingers on the bar so long, Hayden didn't know if he was planning to answer.

"Have you ever been to St. Louis, Hayden?"

"Yes. But it's been years."

"Did you visit the poor area, where the so-called houses aren't much more than shacks, and families are packed in like grain in a sack?"

Suspecting this might hurt to hear, he steeled himself to listen anyway. "No."

"That's where we lived. My pa scratched out a living shoeing horses, fixing wagon wheels, making tools. With ten children, money didn't go far. When Heather came of age, the men came calling, all right. But I'm sure you can guess they weren't the kind of men my mother wanted her to marry—not by a long shot."

What could he say? His mind raced. Just then, Roady and Francis came through the saloon doors, inquisitive expressions on their faces. They spotted Hayden and Morgan and started over.

"What's going on?" Roady asked, plunking his boot on the brass foot rail as Francis stared wide-eyed at the hubbub.

"They're all worked up because of Heather," Hayden replied, keenly mindful that Roady still had an engagement with Heather this afternoon. "She's been getting all sorts of letters. From men asking for her hand. They want her to hurry up and make a decision."

Roady leaned back, craning his neck as if trying to see everyone who was there. "Guess I shouldn't mention I'm taking her on an outing later today."

"Probably not," Morgan said, waving the bartender down.

"Did you see who was over there?" Roady asked, shaking his head. "Ol' man Beaverton! His gray beard down to his belly. He must be fifty-five, if not a day. Isn't he a mite old for Heather?"

Francis laughed. "He don't think so."

Hayden worked to keep his cool, digging deep for some quiet spot in his soul. The conversation he'd had with Heather in the kitchen of the boardinghouse had changed things for them, in his mind, anyway. She'd opened up. Shared intimate memories. He couldn't picture her with Beaverton, Roady, or any of them!

By God, Heather was his! She'd come out to wed him. If he'd had half a brain, they'd be happily married right now. He'd be enjoying her bright conversations, which he missed so much, and starting a whole new life with her—an intimate one, as well. But like the stubborn mule that he was, he'd thrown his chance away. Now one of these idiots could end up with his prize. What if she found someone she liked better? Read a letter and took a liking? He couldn't stop her. And surely, if the man were smart, he'd have her to the preacher before you could say, "Finders, keepers."

June appeared out of the crowd, joining their group.

"Where'd you come from?" Francis asked.

She eyed the rowdy men in the bar, then wedged in between Morgan and Roady, dragging a smile from Heather's brother. "Back door. I heard a few men talking that there was going to be a meeting in here today. I guess word got out and just kept right on going. Looks like all of Y Knot and Pine Grove combined."

Francis whistled, having a good time. "Sure does!"

"It's pretty sickening, actually," she said, gesturing to the men. "Heather sure has 'em worked into a lather."

"I think her appeal has something to do with her being a city gal," Francis offered, rubbing his forehead as he took the excitement in.

Abe finally scooted down to their end of the bar, his face moist with sweat. "Sorry, boys, June, to keep ya waiting. You all want a beer or what?"

"Beers all the way around," June said, counting the nodding faces. "Heather's been good for your business, Abe. You gonna cut her in? I'd say she's earned it."

"I'd feel better if Brandon Crawford were back," Hayden remarked after Abe set a beer in front of each person.

Morgan looked at him. "Who's Brandon Crawford?"

"The sheriff of Y Knot. Has been for a few years. He's away, not quite sure where. Jack Jones is in charge in his absence."

"He went to check on Charity in Denver, is what I heard." Roady almost drained his glass. "And a week after he left, the extra deputy he'd hired on the month before quit and left town. Couldn't stand working with Jack. Can't say as I blame him any."

Hayden nodded. "That's exactly why I wish Brandon would hurry up and get home. Jack's fine if nothing is going on, but . . ."

"Yeah, I have about as much faith in Jack Jones keeping the peace as I would in Francis. No offense, Francis," Roady said. After a moment, he amended his statement. "Actually, I take that back. I'd have more faith in Francis."

Francis had finished his beer and was trying to catch Abe's eye. He heard the comment and grunted proudly.

The group was deep in conversation and didn't notice when Luke McCutcheon, followed by his brothers, Matthew and Mark, strode into the room. Hayden caught Luke's eye and the brothers joined them, crowding into the already cramped space.

"What the devil is going on today?" Luke asked, looking around.

"Last time I saw the Hitching Post this crowded," Matt added, "was the afternoon of the big stock sale of '83."

"I think Miss Heather Stanford should make an appearance here today. Sort of a preview of things to come," the man named Martin shouted.

Matt and Mark looked at each other, eyebrows raised. Luke shook his head in disgust.

Before anyone knew what was up, Hayden

reached down and pulled the revolver from Roady's holster and fired into the air. Bits of debris rained down from the ceiling and the place went dead quiet.

Chapter Twenty-Seven

"Hey, jackasses!" Hayden couldn't help himself as his ire boiled over. "Miss Stanford *isn't* some prize *heifer* or *mare* to be talked about like that." His rage had built to a head and he'd snapped. "Keep a civil tongue in your head when speaking about her, or I might just have to yank it out!"

Raucous laughter erupted in the room. Men backed away as the unkempt man who'd been running his mouth when they'd first come in, stepped forward. He pointed a finger at Hayden, a malevolent glare in his eyes. "You had your chance, Klinkner, and you blew it! You ain't got no claim on that woman, so just get on home with your tail between your legs. You can't come in here and tell us what we can and what we can't be doing. Understand?"

Hayden pushed off the bar and surged through the throng of men, knocking a few over in the process. Intent on humbling this ugly little man, he didn't even see anyone else. Before he reached his prey, however, Roady grabbed his arm and yanked him to a halt. Luke gripped his other. Francis's smile had disappeared and June looked as angry as the rest.

Hayden shrugged off his friends.

Shouts, then a sick-sounding gurgle went up.

Unseen, Morgan had skimmed around the group, circling behind the loudest of the rabble-rousers. With one of his powerful arms wrapped around the man's neck, he leaned back and took him clear off his feet.

Luke pushed through the men toward Morgan as Roady and Francis took another hold of Hayden.

Jack Jones hustled up from the rear of the saloon, both Colt 45s drawn and ready. "What the heck is going on in here?" the deputy shouted. Patches of pink blotched his cheeks, his usual nervous reaction any time a situation got tense.

"It's about time you showed up, Jones," Luke growled. "What were you waiting for? Christmas?"

Jack tried to push the congregation of rowdy men back, but nothing happened.

Hayden reached Morgan as Luke laid a hand on Morgan's shoulder.

"If he dies you could hang, Stanford," Luke said. "Where would that leave your sister?"

Hayden jabbed Martin in the chest, just as Morgan released him. "Get out of town now if you know what's good for you," he growled. The man stumbled back.

Hayden glanced around. "All of you, listen up! Back off where Heather is concerned! She'll be the one to decide when and *if* she's getting married!"

Disgruntled grumbling rippled around the room.

Martin rubbed his throat, a malevolent look in his eyes. "Come on, men! It ain't breaking the law to go over to the boardinghouse and make her pick. Jack Jones can't stop us!"

Matthew and Mark McCutcheon walked slowly toward the saloon doors, planting their feet wide in front of the exit. Roady and Francis followed. Soon Morgan, June, and Luke were there too.

"We'll be sure Jack arrests *anyone* Miss Stanford lodges a complaint against," Hayden shouted. "Understand? Lock you up tight and throw the key away for disturbing the peace. This whole mail-order bride mess has gotten out of control. Now *get!* The bar's closed for one hour."

When Abe's mouth dropped open and he started to protest, Hayden drilled him with a blistering stare. "Closed," he said again.

The batwing doors swished back and forth as the men filed out in silence. Hayden, Morgan, Luke, and the rest watched, then gathered at the bar. Fancy stood on the second-story landing.

The men went quiet. One by one, they turned to stare at Hayden.

"Seems you've created a problem for Y Knot, Hayden," Luke said. "We like our town quiet and peaceful. Safe for our women folk. The last few days, it's been anything but."

It was true. Even though he hadn't written to

St. Louis asking for Heather, his mother had. As long as Heather was single and living at the boardinghouse, he'd never feel completely comfortable that she was safe. "Seems I have."

"Good. I'm glad we see this in the same light."

Hayden was about to say he'd get his courting clothes on when Luke turned and clamped a firm hand on Roady's shoulder. "I guess it's up to you, Guthrie, to clean it up. Seems to have taken a liking to you, too." Morgan nodded.

Shocked, Hayden couldn't think of any way to object without sounding foolish. Several moments passed as if they were waiting on his reaction. "Where are they going to live?" he asked finally. "In the bunkhouse with the rest of the cowboys?"

"We've been talking about just that," Luke said as he picked up his warm beer. "Roady's been with us for years. He's earned some acreage, someplace to build a home and start a family."

When his friend's chest puffed out, Hayden felt the urge to set upon him. *Have they all planned this behind my back?*

Roady grinned mischievously, and his expression said he was up for the challenge. So be it!

"Good luck," he heard himself saying. Just because he sets his sights on her doesn't mean she'll have him. *Or will she?* He cursed himself as a fool and his mouth went dry. All the men nodded, as if the deal were as good as done.

• • •

In her bedroom, Heather sank down onto the slightly worn flowered quilt with a sigh. She unlaced her boots, pulling off first one, then the other. She eyed the stack of mail on her chest of drawers. Eight new posts had arrived today, bringing the total to over thirty—and she hadn't read a single one. She couldn't conjure up a whit of interest for what was written inside. Whether from a foreign prince or the governor of the territory, she wouldn't care. She'd thumbed through the return addresses, hungry for news from home or from Lina in Sweetwater Springs. It was her only way to forget about the fiasco that hung around her like a cold, wet coat.

As she lay back, Mr. Simpson's grouchy expression surfaced in her mind. Poor man! He'd implied several times today she was to blame that his eyesight was deteriorating faster by the day. Too much poor penmanship to read. He'd snapped at her twice, which was so unlike him in the short time they'd been friends. She didn't want to create enemies here in Y Knot, especially if she planned on staying. That was yet to be decided, she reminded herself. If only the men would stop writing her love letters and just leave her alone!

Heather threw her arm over her eyes, concentrating on nothing except the feel of her feather pillow. She had a few minutes to herself before she needed to freshen up for her ride with Roady Guthrie. He'd sent a note to the boardinghouse, letting her know he'd changed their destination since she'd already ridden out to the Holcombs' with Hayden. He had a surprise in mind, and was being secretive about it.

Disappointment at not seeing Evie again was chased away by a feeling of adventure and experiencing something new. She'd done her laundry and ironing yesterday and planned to wear her pink cotton dress, perfect for today. She'd braid the matching pink ribbon Sally had given her for her last birthday into her hair.

There was a light rap on the door.

"Yes?"

"I hate to disturb you," Lou said. "But there's another man here to see you. He's waiting on the front porch, making sure every man around notices he's here."

"Who is it? Do I know him?"

"I don't think so. I don't know him and he said the two of you have not met. I would've sent him away, but didn't know if you were expecting him before your outing with Mr. Guthrie—and because he has a beautiful bouquet of roses to give you."

"Thank you, Lou. Will you please tell him I'm not interested." *My! Don't I sound like a spoiled princess! As much as I love flowers, nothing could entice me to sit and chat with a stranger.* "I only have a short time before Mr. Guthrie comes to pick me up and I'm not even dressed."

"Of course, Heather. I'll have Drit take care of it. Maybe this young feller will get the message."

"Thank you."

Heather went to the porcelain pitcher and bowl and washed her face, then brushed her teeth and combed and styled her hair. With only a few minutes remaining, she donned her dress and pulled her boots back on. They were her only pair, comfortable or not.

Thinking of Roady, she took one last look in the mirror. Satisfied, she reached for her shawl, folded and ready to go on the dresser. Roady was nice enough, she thought, and handsome, too. Where Hayden's golden hair curled enticingly around his tanned face, Roady's was dark and thick, cut neatly around his ears and neck. Where Hayden's eyes coaxed her to share secrets she held dear in her heart, Roady's playful gaze made her smile and relax.

The two men were as different as the sun and moon, but the same too, in a charming sort of way. The few times she'd met him, Roady Guthrie seemed agreeable and witty. If she tried hard, knowing she would like to have children of her own someday, she could see herself married to him, the days and years passing happily.

Several babies in her arms.

Surprised at the thought, she paused. Was

Hayden interested at all? No, she was sure he wasn't. She had to get that through her head. And especially through her heart. If he were, he'd have made it known. A knock at the front door, then the rich timbre of Roady's voice resonated all the way up to her room. She'd best start getting on with her life. Life *without* Hayden.

Lou must have said something funny because Roady's deep laughter rolled up the stairs, making her smile. Passing in front of the mirror, she caught her reflection and noticed that her cheeks had actually turned pink without having to pinch them. Maybe, just maybe, this outing would be more enjoyable than she'd first thought. At least she should give Roady a chance.

Chapter Twenty-Eight

After his friends left, Hayden went outside and leaned against the rail, feeling lower than he had in days. In five minutes, the place would open back up and the men hanging around town would materialize from the alleys and shadows and get back to drinking. He couldn't stop them, and he really didn't want to. He'd just wanted them to cool off. Think with a clear head.

He looked left and his jaw tightened. As anticipated, Roady pulled up to the boardinghouse in a rented buggy. Hayden knew he shouldn't stand there watching like some lovesick pup, but his feet weren't listening to his brain. He wanted to see Heather. Watch how she responded to his friend. The fact that the McCutcheons would give Roady a parcel of land had branded his belly like a lance straight from the forge.

Nervous, he walked around to the opening in the rail and stepped down onto the dusty street, going to his gelding's side.

What's taking them so long?

He lifted his stirrup and checked his cinch, just for something to do.

Heather's laughter made him look up and over the back of his horse. He was too far away to hear what Roady had said, but the cowhand was handing her up into the seat. It was only a moment until he was in the seat beside her and they started off, heading straight for the saloon.

Damn. If they were going out to the Holcombs', Roady would have had to turn around right away and head east. Now it would only be moments until they saw him standing here, watching. Should he make a dash for the saloon?

"Hayden," Roady called, making a point to draw him to Heather's attention. *The skunk.* He'd be sure to pay him back the next chance he got.

His so-called friend pulled the buggy to a halt with Heather on his side of the street.

He walked out nonchalantly to the side of the buggy. "Roady, Heather. Going for a ride?"

She smiled. The golden flecks in her emerald eyes deepened.

He had to force his gaze over to Roady, sitting next to her like a proud peacock. "Thought you two were going to the Holcombs'? Isn't that the opposite direction?"

"That was the old plan. I have something new in mind since Heather was just there with you, not two days ago. Don't want her to be bored."

Roady slid Heather a sideways glance that was ripe with mischief, causing Hayden's blood to boil.

Heather smiled. "And just what exactly is that plan, may I ask?"

"No, you may not." Roady winked at her. "I intend it to be a surprise."

Roady clucked to the sorrel in the harness and the animal trotted off.

Hayden stood in the middle of the road with his hands dangling at his sides. As he turned back for his horse, the musician he'd seen in the boardinghouse came walking up the street, the mandolin in his hands. He strummed a few chords and began,

> *Long Ike and Sweet Betsy got married, of course,*
> *But Ike, getting jealous, obtained a divorce,*
> *While Betsy, well satisfied, said with a shout,*
> *"Good-bye, you big lummox, I'm glad you backed out!"*

Fed up, Hayden strode over to the man. His two-tone pants were as ragged as the rest of him. "If you've got something to say, spit it out!"

"Nope. Nothing at all. Just passing the time and singing a song."

"That may be true, but leave me alone. I don't appreciate your talent."

Heather squashed her desire to turn around and see if Hayden was still standing in the street, watching. The buggy traveled down Main toward Half Hitch Street, the road that forked onto Creek Street—where the Klinkners lived. How were Ina and Norman? Was Mr. Klinkner doing better with his crutches? She wished she'd had a chance to ask Hayden, but every sensible thought had flown from her mind the moment she'd spotted him in front of the saloon. The buggy bounced hard and she realized she probably should be making some kind of conversation. She looked up to find Roady watching her carefully, a mysterious gleam in his eyes.

"Two bits for your thoughts," he said, which caught her off guard. He offered a semblance of a smile. "Pondering about Hayden?"

How could she answer without telling a lie? Still, his humorous way of saying it put a smile on her lips. "Well, sort of, I guess. I was thinking about his mother and father mostly. I hope Mr. Klinkner is doing better. And I worry about Ina, too. I hope she isn't working so hard that she gets sick. Dr. Handerhoosen said there have been a couple of cases of influenza in Pine Grove. I wouldn't want that." The road had smoothed out and Roady urged the horse on, the air whipping at the strands of her braid.

"No, we sure wouldn't."

The vivid blue sky seemed to go on and on. Turning her face up to the sun, Heather enjoyed the warmth on her skin. She was happy not to be in the boardinghouse helping with the supper preparations and setting the table. Lou had insisted she take the time off.

"Where're we going?"

He looked her way, the dark slash of his brow tipped. "We'll be there soon enough. It's something a lady with your sophistication will enjoy."

"All right." *What on earth can be out here?* She tried to stay her curiosity. Relaxing even more, her thoughts strayed to Hayden, and his being at the saloon—again. Well, it wasn't her problem if he was a drinker. Morgan had mentioned meeting Hayden at the saloon several other times as well. She'd sworn never to marry a man with her father's taste for whiskey. She should be happy the way things had turned out.

The road started an uphill climb. Roady pulled the horse down to a walk, letting him catch his breath.

"You're considerably quiet for a girl."

She straightened in her seat. "I guess." She just couldn't think of anything to talk about. It was absurd. Her mind was completely empty of topics to discuss besides Hayden. She marveled at how easily their conversations flowed. Finally she said, "It's beautiful weather. Is Montana always this warm in the summertime?"

"Pretty much."

At the top of the rise, the land leveled and stretched out as far as the eye could see. Roady slowed the horse even more until the buggy stopped.

"Here we are." He got out and went around to her side, extending his hand. Taking it, she tried to feel the spark she did whenever she took Hayden's hand. She smiled into his attractive face, so sincere and caring. Any girl would consider herself fortunate to have such a charming escort.

On the ground, Heather straightened her dress. There was nothing out of the ordinary that she recognized.

He laughed, and a warm feeling took her by surprise.

"I can see you're wondering what we're doing out here. Well, just be patient a bit longer and I'll show you." He folded her hand around the crook of his arm. He looked at the western horizon and then to the north for several long moments, as if gauging his location. Then they strolled into the wide-open plains, the brown grass blowing around their legs and feet. White, puffy clouds hanging low in the sky drew Heather's attention. In St. Louis she never had such a view, and if she did the air looked hazy and brown from smoke.

A small squirrel-like animal, but without the long tail, darted out in front of them.

Heather gasped and clutched Roady's arm.

"Just a little prairie dog. He's more scared of you than you are of him."

Taking hold of herself, she nodded. Of course it was just a little prairie dog, but little prairie dogs were scarce in St. Louis. And the landscape was so quiet out here. She glanced back at the buggy, and the way they'd come. "I'm fine. Just different from what I'm used to."

"I bet. The sun never sets in the city, I've heard."

She swallowed, still not understanding why he'd brought her into the field full of blowing grass. He stopped and pointed down. A layer of rocks, perhaps left by a volcano, was interspersed with the foliage. He bent down and pushed some of the dried stalks of oats away. Presumably not finding what he'd been looking for, he stood, walked a couple of feet to her right, bent again and felt around.

"Look here."

Heather followed. She took hold of her long skirt, then squatted as ladylike as she could. She bent closer. "What is it?"

"See?" With a work-roughened finger, he traced something in one of the rocks. "This here is a fossil. From thousands of years ago. If you look just right, you'll see a fish shape."

She sucked in an excited breath. "Roady! How wonderful!"

She traced the shape with her finger, delight warming her breeze-cooled skin. "Yes. Here's a fin, and sort of a long, snake-like tail."

The indentation was not more than four inches

long, but to Heather the intriguing fossil was better than a treasure chest filled with gold. "When I was just a little girl, my parents would take us down to the city center when the traveling exposition came through," she said, looking over at him. "Morgan or Travis would hold my hand so I wouldn't get lost. Mother and Father carried the younger children."

Roady's eyes warmed.

She was unable to hide her pleasure as the memories came rushing back. "Thank you for being so thoughtful."

Roady pushed himself to a standing position. He was hatless and the wind tousling his hair made him look incredibly handsome. He stretched out his arm and turned a slow circle. "I'm told all this used to be a vast ocean bed," he said, the rich timbre of his voice holding a bit of awe. "Imagine that." He began walking. "Come on. There's a few more over here."

When she followed, several loud barking squeaks went up, halting her.

Laughing, Roady pointed to some mounded humps of earth in the distance, scattered across the grassland. "That's prairie dog town. Hundreds of 'em. Maybe even thousands. The closer you get, the louder they become. It's their warning system. If you're real quiet and can sneak up on 'em, you might even see some of their young'uns this time of year."

He waited until she was at his side and took her hand again. "I don't want you to sprain your ankle on this uneven ground."

Heather smiled, enjoying their walk. Maybe the task would take some doing to get over Hayden, but look at what Roady had done just for her. She was grateful. Could she be a cowboy's wife? Was he even interested in her that way?

Chapter Twenty-Nine

Two days later, Hayden sat by the lamplight in his small home, staring at the sheet of paper before him. He couldn't rid himself of the image of Roady and Heather in the buggy.

There was no mistaking her happy smile. And the way Roady carried on. You'd think the two had known each other for years.

Hayden picked up his pencil for the tenth time, and tapped the lead nervously on the tabletop, not caring if it made any marks. If he didn't do something, and quick, Heather would be lost to him forever. The ticking of the clock sounded louder and louder. Just how did one go about writing a love letter, after the way his mother had botched things up?

Just start!

Write something!

Dear Heather. He picked up his hand. Stared at the print. It was big and sloppy. In his line of work, he didn't get much practice. Hell! Heather wasn't going to judge his style; it would be his words that mattered.

He wadded up the sheet and started over.

My dearest Heather.

There, that was better.

I know we did not have a good start. I am sorry. I wish things had been d. i. f. f. e. r—*he paused, sounding out the difficult word*—e. n. t. Different. But what is done is done. I am writing you this letter because I would like to be considered as one of your suitors. When making your choice for a husband, please know that I, Hayden Klinkner, am the first in line.

If you are wondering if this is really me, and not my mother again, I will tell you that your sparkling eyes on our moonlight ride out to the Holcombs' have been difficult to forget. I had to look away several times because I was so overcome by your beauty. As you shared with me about your brothers and sisters, I kept thinking there was not another girl as lovely as you. You completely stole my heart.

If you have no desire to wed, I will try to accept your decision gracefully, although it will be the hardest thing I ever do.

I will be waiting for your answer.
All my love,
Hayden Klinkner

Post Script: While working at the mill, Morgan mentioned to me your dislike of your father's drinking. I do not blame you for those feelings. I want you to know that my nightly trips to the saloon have only been to relieve my loneliness. Living and working at the mill, and with my parents, good people that they are, did not afford me much time socializing. The house is usually quiet, and out of boredom, I go into town. I have always had a one-beer limit. I hope you understand. If we marry, I vow to stay at home with my wife every night. And I am a believer. I love you.

Completely spent, Hayden lowered the pencil and read what he'd written. If that didn't win Heather's heart, nothing would. It wasn't poetry, but it was him and it was sincere. Nothing more. A month ago, she'd been willing to take a chance on a hardworking lumberman. Hopefully, Roady or another of the other men vying for her hand hadn't changed her mind.

He carefully folded the sheet and slipped it in an envelope, thinking all the while that if she said yes it might be only a matter of days before . . .

He glanced around his place with a critical eye. It was small. Hadn't been built with a wife and family in mind. More or less one large room with a bed in one corner, but was the only way to have some privacy as he'd grown older. Instinctively, he'd known his mother's heart would have shattered if he'd moved totally away. As always, the rusty old memory of his mother crying in his father's arms on that snowy Christmas Eve momentarily wounded him.

So six years ago, without his father's help because he'd wanted to do it alone, he'd built this place and connected it to his parents' house with a covered boardwalk through his mother's garden. Only one room with a fireplace and two windows—one with a view of the river. Besides the bed, and a bookshelf filled with books, there was a table and two chairs. Not much, but cozy. If Heather said yes, he'd add a kitchen if she wanted, or if she preferred to cook up at the family house, that would be fine with him.

The envelope was still blank. Mr. Simpson would have the news all over town the moment he saw the return address. Did he care? Would it stop him?

No!

He'd risk everything for Heather. Besides, once she read his words, she'd seek him out. Warmth pulsed up his body as he imagined the meeting, the kiss, the wedding night. Happiness was just a day or two away.

"What is *wrong* with him?" Roady stomped to the livery window and looked out on the dark town, stubbornly refusing to budge. June sat quietly at her desk. "I never considered Hayden Klinkner a coward—or a dunce!"

Morgan, who'd been silent up to now, stepped forward. "I don't know," he said, feeling the responsibility of his sister's future, or lack of it, fall squarely in his lap. "I should have put a stop to this foolish idea the moment Chance suggested it. Maybe his wife doesn't know what she's talking about. Heather is being pretty closemouthed, too."

Chance stiffened at the remark. "It's not Evie's fault. She's just trying to do what's right by Heather. By now, if it were me losing Evie, I'd be at her doorstep day and night. Maybe someone should talk to him. Just making him jealous isn't working."

Luke lounged against one stall door, stroking the neck of the docile occupant, listening. "He'll make a move when the heat gets hot enough."

Roady turned but stayed where he was. "Luke, I don't like leading her on. Don't get me wrong. If I believed I had a chance, and she wasn't in love with Hayden, I'd throw my hat into the ring. Give it my best ride. Still, I most certainly don't want to be married to someone who's in love with another man. Nope, not for me, fellas. What if she just *thinks* she's fallen for me? We had a darn nice time on our outing. Then what am I supposed to do? Propose?"

He looked away quickly, making Morgan think that his new friend just may have fallen for his sister in spite of himself. Too much was at stake. What if Hayden didn't come around, Roady fell for her, but she married another suitor from the stacks and stacks of letters she'd been receiving? Anything was possible. "This is getting out of hand," Morgan said, challenging Luke. "It's my sister we're talking about. Roady could be right. I'm not going to let her heart be broken again. It's not right what she suffered when she first arrived in Y Knot. She lived through that pretending the disaster hadn't ripped her heart out. This is only making that worse."

"We just have to make Hayden a little more uncomfortable," Luke said. "Make him think you're going to propose—soon."

"And how am I supposed to make him believe that without actually letting Heather know my intentions? I'm telling you, this is getting too hot for even *me*. I like a practical joke now and then, you all know I do, but this is far above and beyond."

"We have to stay the course," Chance said. "They were out at our house. It felt right. The lovelorn looks were flying faster than the geese in the fall."

June stood, the indecision in her eyes. She flashed him an apologetic expression before saying, "I'm siding with Luke and Chance on this. If we stop now, Heather may be brokenhearted for the rest of her life. Settling. It's like a curse word to every woman on the face of this earth." She quickly held her hand up to Roady. "No offense, of course, Roady. It's just that no one knows how a heart falls for one and not another. Doesn't mean one man is better than the next, it's just some unknown phenomenon of our innermost being."

Morgan hid his smile. He admired June, although he'd never let that spitfire know. Her thick chestnut hair was always clean and shiny, something rare for a farrier, and the mischievous look in her eyes made him wonder—much too often—what was going on in her head. He wiggled his jaw, testing its soreness, thankful that his tooth had gone back to normal. She liked to act like one of the men. In her jeans and thick flannel shirt, she dressed like one too. But the way the clothes fit her body, she was anything but. All woman underneath. He liked her, which surprised him considering their scuffle in the hay and his sore jaw.

Roady harrumphed. "Keep it simple, June."

"I'm just saying, I also think Hayden and Heather were meant to be a couple. Things got bungled with Ina muddling things, but that doesn't mean they can't end up where they should. Then again, without Ina, maybe Heather wouldn't even be here."

Luke meandered toward the middle of the group. "Fine. We'll give the plan one more shot. Here's what I think we should do."

Chapter Thirty

Early the next morning, Hayden lurked inside the leather shop, watching through the grimy plate-glass window as his letter weighed his pocket down like a stone. He needed to make sure Heather was nowhere near Lichtenstein's next door, before he went in and posted it.

"Whatcha watching for?" Mr. Herrick, the owner of the store asked. "Looks like yer hidin' out."

Hayden whipped around. He'd completely forgotten about the man, even though he'd heard the noises as the shopkeeper had gone about stuffing his beat-up iron stove with wood and starting a fire. The man was dressed in his usual denim jeans covered by short leather chaps for protection. Mr. Herrick's store was always open at five a.m. sharp. Didn't matter if rain was pouring down or they were in the midst of a blizzard.

"No, not hiding. Brought this in for mending, and thought I saw someone I knew coming down the boardwalk." He held out a beat-up old halter, ready to fall apart.

Mr. Herrick chuckled. "Your pa replaced that ol' thing last month when I told him buying a new one would be cheaper." He tottered to the window, pushing his glasses up on his nose. "Still pretty early out there. I don't see anyone."

In a rush to explain himself, Hayden pointed at the only person on the street. Berta May, unlocking the door to her sewing shop.

"That's just Berta May? You knowed her for as long as I have." He paused. "You feeling all right, boy?"

Hayden didn't have to turn to know Mr. Herrick was staring at him as if he'd lost all logic. He rubbed his eye. "I guess I just got something in my eye is all."

"I think you got some fluff in your brain. A good strong cup of coffee will clear out all the cobwebs."

Hayden didn't dare leave the window. He kept glancing out every so often as he flipped the quarter over in his fingers. Heather must be coming out of the boardinghouse soon. She was due at Doc Handerhoosen's. "That sounds good. Think I will."

Mr. Herrick gave him another disturbed sideward glance before starting for the stove. "It'll be awhile. Ain't started perking yet."

"Fine. Fine. I'm in no rush."

Lenore Saffelberg came marching down the street, her usual grumpy expression plastered on her face. He assumed she was going to the restaurant inside the Cattlemen's Hotel where she worked. Pretty early for a waitress.

The door to the boardinghouse opened and Heather came out.

Hayden's breath caught. He recognized her yellow dress from when she was living with them. She had a basket, the handle draped over her arm. All sorts of feelings surged inside him. What if she said no after reading his letter? Would she? Could she? Maybe with all the attention she'd been getting lately, she'd completely forgotten about him.

She arrived at the boardwalk just as Lenore was passing. They stopped. Chatted. He'd never taken a liking to Lenore. She was too nosy for his taste. Her sharp tongue could slice a man in two before he even knew what hit him.

"That's the new gal, Heather."

Surprised by the sudden voice in his ear, Hayden lurched forward, knocking his forehead hard against the glass. The window reverberated. "Don't sneak up on me like that."

"I ain't sneaking, I'm walking." Mr. Herrick's eyes narrowed. He'd put two and two together. "But I don't need to be telling you about her, now do I?"

"No, you don't."

The women parted and Heather looked both ways on the quiet street before crossing. Picking up her hem to keep her dress clean, she crossed and disappeared into the doctor's office, but not before Hayden noted how beautiful she looked this morning, or how her movements reminded him of a swan. How long should he wait to be sure she was busy doing her chores? Five minutes? Ten?

He diverted his attention to the saddle on display in front of him and inspected the tooling while his mind raced. He heard Mr. Herrick puttering around behind the counter. *Enough!* He had to get this done.

Hayden set his hat on his head and tugged it down. When he turned, he ran straight into the leather smith, dumping both cups of coffee straight to the floor.

"What on earth has you so buggered up, son? My gosh." Shaking his head, he set the near-to-empty cups down, eying the mess at their feet.

"Sorry!" Hayden tossed the halter onto a saddle and grabbed his handkerchief from his pocket, shoving the piece of white cotton at him. "I need to go," he said, rushing for the door. "I decided I don't want any coffee after all."

"What about the halter?"

"Keep it!"

Pulling himself together, Hayden slipped into Lichtenstein's. Mr. Simpson looked up from the counter. He gave Hayden a pleasant smile. "Mornin', Hayden. How's your pa doing?"

"Good. He's itching to get back to work, but of course Doc and my ma won't allow it."

"That's good to hear. Can I help you find anythin'?"

Hayden swallowed. Moved toward the counter. "No, actually I'm just here to send a post."

"Lotta that going on lately." The clerk's voice was hard. "All this namby-pamby love letter business. I'm happy to post a 'real' correspondence. In fact, I'm jumping with joy!"

Slapping the letter down before he lost his nerve, Hayden felt as if he were facing a firing squad.

When Mr. Simpson read to whom the letter was addressed, the store clerk's lips thinned. He lifted his head. Through his spectacles, his gaze pierced Hayden with a glare. "You too?" he asked angrily. "It was *you* who started this whole business in the first place. My fingers are worn to the bone from sorting mail, and my eyes are ruby red—jist like a chicken's—by the time my day is over." He pointed to a stack of mail in the corner. "See what you done."

"Not me, Mr. Simpson. You're forgetting about Chance Holcomb. He sent for a bride first. If it weren't for him, my mother wouldn't have met Evie and taken a liking to her. He put the notion of a mail-order bride in her head. Otherwise, none of this would've happened. If you need to place blame, look to him." *And if things turn out like I'm hoping, I'll thank him later.*

"That'll be six cents."

As Hayden fished the coins from his pocket, the door opened. Before he could turn, Heather's voice called out in a cheerful greeting. "Good morning, Mr. Simpson, the doctor needs a bottle of iodine. I suspect iodine would be next to ice cream if you had any, and since you don't—"

"Jam," Mr. Simpson barked out irritably, crossing his arms over his chest as he looked back and forth between the two.

As if startled by the clerk's tone, Heather pulled up short, her smile fading away.

Hayden slipped the hat from his head. The action drew her attention. Her expression softened and, if he wasn't fooling himself, longing warmed her eyes. His heart picked up tempo as he prayed the grumpy clerk wouldn't rat him out.

She gripped her hands together in front of her.

"Iodine is next to the jam," Mr. Simpson said again as if she hadn't heard him the first time. "You know where that is?"

Heather nodded. "Y-Yes, I do."

She looked happy. The question was, why was she so? She appeared rested and her cheeks had a healthy sheen. Had her lashes always been so dark and long? Had she gotten good news from home? Had she and Roady grown closer? Were his efforts all for naught?

"Heather," he said, walking over to her even though his insides quaked. "You sure look pretty today." She blushed. Oh, how he wanted to pull her into his arms and kiss her! Then he'd snatch back the letter he'd just paid six cents to post, and give it to her. Get this torture over with. Once she read his words and knew what was in his heart, she'd comply. She'd come all this way just to marry him, hadn't she?

"Thank you," she said. "What brings you to town so early?"

Mr. Simpson coughed conspicuously.

When Hayden reached over and tucked a wayward strand of hair behind her ear, she didn't pull away. Tongue-tied, he felt his heart beat against his chest as he struggled to get the words out without sounding stupid. "I'm just in doing errands."

Heather flushed and glanced away when he moved a little closer. "How're your father's spirits holding up?" she asked. "Dr. Handerhoosen says he's healing nicely."

"Grumpy. Ma has her hands full. But all in all, he's doing well."

"I'm so glad to hear that. And the order for the Night Owl? Will you be finished on time?"

"With time to spare, thanks to you. Morgan is a great help. I'm planning on asking him to stay on when we're finished. Do you think he will?"

"I don't know. That's for him to say."

The clomping of Mr. Simpson's boots walking in their direction broke the spell.

"Here." He handed a small bottle to Heather. When she just stared at it, he added, "The iodine."

"Oh, yes. Thank you."

"I'll put it on Doc's tab," the clerk mumbled as he stalked off.

Uncertainty fluttered across her face. "Nice seeing you, Hayden. I'll be getting back to work now."

"My pleasure, Heather." *I hope, if things go as planned, I'll be seeing a lot more of you once you read my letter.*

Chapter Thirty-One

As the day drew to an end, Heather gathered her things to return to the boardinghouse. Finished with her duties at the mercantile, she looked forward to a little time alone to ponder her meeting with Hayden and her last outing with Roady. What did any of it mean? Her head hurt from thinking so much.

The only good news was that Mr. Klinkner was healing well and the order for the Night Owl would be completed on time. That was a great comfort.

Her basket now filled with the supplies Lou had requested she bring home, she waited for Mr. Simpson so she could say good-bye. As the clerk came up the narrow aisle, the cowhand she'd seen speaking with Hayden outside the mill came through the door.

He quickly doffed his hat. "Miss."

"Hello." She instantly liked him. He reminded her of Peter, her mischievous brother whom she adored, and hoped he wasn't another man who wanted to marry her.

"You're Miss Stanford."

"That's right. And you're . . ."

"I'm Francis. I work for the McCutcheons. I know Hayden real well and I've met your brother. I live with Roady in the bunkhouse, although he'll move out when he gets his house built. Then—"

Mr. Simpson cleared his throat. "Is there something you wanted, Francis?"

That broke the young cowboy's attention. He stammered for a moment. "Actually, yes," he said. "Roady is watching the herd today and tonight, but he wanted me to come into town and let you know he's planning on taking you to the Twilight Singers performance at the gazebo. You heard about it? The gazebo is behind the Biscuit Barrel."

"Yes, I've been there."

"Has someone already asked you? He wanted me to find out."

She shook her head. "I haven't been asked."

"Good. Then plan on going with him?"

Mr. Simpson sighed loudly. "What does this store look like? Cupid's corner?"

Heather smiled, although it was not from the heart. "Please tell Roady I'd be delighted."

A huge grin split Francis's face. "I will." He stepped back and held the door.

"Wait up there, missy!"

Heather turned.

Mr. Simpson drilled her with a look. "Don't you dare go without all these letters."

"I don't want them, Mr. Simpson. I don't even want to look through them."

"It's my duty to deliver the US mail to the person the letters are addressed to. It's a federal offense not to. What you do with them is up to you."

When he tried to hand them to her, she stepped back. "Will you see if there's any correspondence from St. Louis or Sweetwater Springs?" She beseeched him with her eyes. "Then throw the rest away."

Grumbling, he flipped through the dozen or so posts and came forward with one. "From Sweetwater Springs. Mind you, I'm keeping the rest in case you change your mind."

Taking it, Heather bid both men thank-you and good-bye and hurried across the street to the boardinghouse. The parlor was empty, and she was thankful. All she could think about was Lina's letter. She closed her door and sank onto her bed, opening the envelope to withdraw the vanilla-colored notepaper. With a sigh and a heavy heart, Heather began to read.

Dear Heather,

I read your letter and wanted to burst into tears. How disappointing that Hayden (as you call him so familiarly) does not want to marry. I can read what you did NOT write, my dear friend, and that is that you have feelings for Hayden Klinkner. Although you write with your usual determination, I'm sure your heart must be hurting, which makes mine hurt for you too.

There is not a Catholic church in Sweetwater Springs, Heather. Neither Mr. Barrett nor Trudy thought to mention that in their letters. Normally, I would rush straight to church and light a candle for you. Now I will just say a special prayer to the Blessed Mother for you to find a loving husband—either because Hayden's heart becomes open to you or because you find another man to love.

My arrival in Sweetwater Springs and subsequent wedding took place in the midst of a downpour. Mr. Barrett showed up with his son and some flowers for me, which would have been romantic if most of the blooms had not fallen off by the time I received the bouquet. However, I appreciated the gesture and have pressed the one remaining flower between the pages of my Bible.

My marriage is proving more challenging than I expected. Mr. Barrett and his son are just as Trudy described. They have the most beautiful green eyes, although an air of sorrow clings to both of them. I already love little Adam like my own son.

Our dear Trudy has been such a comfort. She and Seth attended our wedding and drove me home in their covered wagon, since Mr. Barrett does not have a vehicle of any kind. She sent us home with enough prepared meals and baked goods to last several days. Yesterday, she showed up with a gift of chickens and some crocheted doilies. I am sure you remember her beautiful handwork. We are so blessed to have Trudy and Evie to lean on. We did not know Evie well, but now you have a chance to build a beautiful friendship with her. Please pass on my regards and best wishes for her marriage to Mr. Holcomb.

I am so proud of you for making an excellent chicken dinner. Hopefully the memory of such a wonderful repast will stay in Mr. Klinkner's mind, making him think of you at mealtime. They do say the way to a man's heart is through his stomach . . .

Write me more details about what you are doing to provide for yourself and what men (I'm sure there are many) are courting you.

Sincerely,
Lina Barrett

• • •

Two long days had come and gone. Hayden was angry and agitated. He jerked the chain around the log, tightening the shackle with force. Nothing mattered anymore. Heather had gotten his letter. She'd read it. Knew what was in his heart—and yet, *hadn't responded.*

At least I know where I stand. His heart felt scorched; his insides, stony. Since mailing the letter, he hadn't had the nerve to go into town, telling Morgan for the past two evenings he was tired or he wanted to visit with his pa. Of course, everyone still kept him abreast of Heather's comings and goings. Morgan especially seemed intent on mentioning her name almost every other word.

Morgan glanced over. "You gonna get into town tonight? It's that—"

"I *know* what tonight is," Hayden snapped. "The same as every other last Tuesday of every month of the summer!"

Morgan's jaw clenched and his expression went dark. "Don't take out your frustrations on me. I'm only bringing the subject up because your mother asked for help getting the surrey ready and hitching the horses. She wants to take your pa. She can't do it on her own."

Damn. He'd forgotten. Every waking moment he'd spent waiting on Heather, then trying to figure out why she hadn't responded. His mother's request had slipped his mind.

"Forget it! I'll do it," Morgan added brusquely.

Heck! He didn't want to see Heather. Especially now that he'd told her he loved her, and proposed. She would probably laugh all the way to the altar—with Roady. June had been out earlier, needed some kindling. Strange really, since she usually split her own. Thanks to her, he practically knew when Heather went to the necessary. Seemed the skunk cowboy had been dogging her steps all day today, from one workplace to the other.

I think they just like rubbing the situation in my face.

Morgan watched him with a sour expression. "I'll hitch up and drive them," Hayden said. "You go on. I'm sure your friends are waiting."

Morgan shrugged. "So you'll be there for sure?"

"I *said* I would."

"All right. Tomorrow we make the first delivery to Pine Grove. I'll be here early."

Hayden nodded. "I'll see you tonight. We can talk about it then."

Chapter Thirty-Two

"He's coming. Bringing Ina and Norman in the surrey," Morgan said to the group gathered for a last-minute strategy meeting in the livery. Luke had yet to show up. June's encouraging smile did little to settle his nerves.

Roady rubbed his palms on his pants as he glanced around. He pursed his lips and actually gave a little start when the barn cat rubbed against his boot. Chance and Francis chuckled. "My invitation to take Heather to see the singers, and then dogging her heels today, should have brought Hayden running. I have a bad feeling about all this."

Francis looked up from his whittling. "It'll be fine, Roady. If not, you'll end up with a pretty wife."

"Don't like it at all." Roady's usual calm demeanor was slightly panicked.

"Nothing's going to go wrong," Chance said. "Heather just thinks this is an evening out—that's all. It's Hayden who's going to think it's more. With our help, he'll think you're ready to pop the question to his gal." He walked over and clamped Roady on the shoulder. "Just be your charming self. We'll do the rest." Chance looked over to June. "What time is it, anyway? I need to get back out to the ranch and fetch Evie."

• • •

A knock brought Heather out of her concentration. She dotted her *i* and looked at her letter to Lina. "Yes?" she called distractedly.

"Are you ready, Heather?" Lou asked through the door. "Roady should be here any time. I just wanted to let you know it's getting late. It's almost four now."

"Thank you. I'll be right out. I have a few last-minute things I need to finish."

Heather quickly wrote a final sentence to Lina's letter and signed it. How she depended on her friends! Lina's words had bolstered her spirits. It was true. She *was* blessed. She'd come to love this small Montana town. She couldn't imagine ever living in St. Louis again. She missed her family, but she was meant to be here. Maybe she could persuade her mother to come out and bring the girls.

After the ink dried, she carefully folded the note and slipped it into the envelope. Lina Barrett, General Delivery, Sweetwater Springs, she wrote carefully. Everything sounded so lovely there. Although Lina hadn't said too much about her situation with her new husband, Jonah, Heather wondered from the tone of the letter if things were worse than Lina was letting on.

My marriage is proving more challenging than I expected. What exactly did that mean? Challenging? In what way? Nervous energy moved

Heather to the window. She looked down on the street, which was busier than normal with townsfolk walking toward the Biscuit Barrel and beyond.

What if Mr. Barrett were the kind of man to mistreat her friend? Living in the bad part of St. Louis, Heather had seen signs of that all too often. She didn't want that nightmare for Lina. No, she wouldn't think that. Trudy would never recommend Lina to Mr. Barrett if he'd been anything but a good, hardworking man. And Trudy knew of Lina's penchant for children, even stepchildren. Heather had to keep believing that or she'd go crazy with worry.

A shout from outside drew her attention back to the street. A group of men were talking and laughing, and one must have yelled. With a jolt of excitement, she saw Klinkner's surrey coming down the street with Hayden driving, and his parents in the back. Almost directly in front of the boardinghouse now, he glanced up at her window and her breath caught. Their gazes locked. The angry expression on his face rocked her. She gasped. Pulled back from the window.

Why? *Why is he angry?* When they'd met in the mercantile, he'd been so kind. Said she looked pretty. Held her gaze so long she had hoped he'd changed his mind. Now, she didn't know what to think. If his disturbing expression meant anything—it was that she'd never be his. What happened to change him so drastically?

She turned and squeezed her eyes closed, leaning her back against the flowered wallpaper. She'd been holding out hope, praying for a miracle.

Tapping sounded on her door. "He's here, Heather," Lou called. "Roady's waiting on the porch."

With a surge of hope, Heather realized Hayden had seen Roady coming for her. *Is he jealous? Stop! Don't think about him!* If Hayden wasn't interested, he wouldn't care about her being with Roady. He'd been truthful from the start. It was just that she'd hoped so badly that he would change.

"Heather? Did you hear me?"

"Yes, Lou. I'm coming right now."

Lou's receding footsteps gave Heather a moment to pull her emotions together, take hold of her overactive imagination. She glanced in the mirror. "You *will* have a good time today," she said, pointing at her reflection. "Hayden isn't being mean to you. He never, *ever,* led you to believe you were anything to him. Be kind to Roady. Give him a chance. He just might be the one God has chosen for you!"

But even as she said the words, her heart ached.

Hayden drove past the Biscuit Barrel in a haze of anger. *Why did I glance at her window?* he chastised himself. Seeing her had been more painful than a kick from Stonewall.

Driving the surrey as close to the gazebo as he could get, he parked under a tall grove of alders to keep the setting sun from beating down on his father. Norman wouldn't have much of a view, but at least he'd be able to hear the singers putting on their show. Hayden set the brake and climbed out.

"Are you staying, Ma?" She really needed to get out and socialize a little too. She'd been stuck at the mill tending to his pa all this time. When she hesitated, he said, "Come on. It'll do you good."

Norman chuckled. "Go on, woman. You've been nursing me for over two weeks. I could use a little respite from your mother-henning."

Ina harrumphed. "When you put it like that, how can I refuse?" She held out her hand to Hayden, and he helped her to the ground.

She fluffed her skirt and fiddled with her hat. "Go on, Hayden. I can make my own way. I hope to see Clare McCutcheon. I heard she and Flood got back into town yesterday."

"Who told you that?"

"June. When she was out yesterday for kindling."

"Yeah. June."

Ina gave him a long look. "Is everything all right, son? You've been particularly quiet these last few days. Is something bothering you?"

"Nope. Nothing at all." *Just my whole world has gone cockeyed.*

"You sure?" She reached up and touched his cheek just like she used to do when he was a small boy. His heart swelled. She'd meant to help. But bringing Heather into his life had just about ruined him. Looking over her head into the small crowd, he saw Roady with Heather on his arm. Jack Jones stood off to the side, a bitter expression plastered on his face, as well as several other men. He wasn't the only one feeling the strain.

He leaned down and kissed his mother's cheek. Too bad he and Heather wouldn't be giving her the grandbabies she craved. "I'm sure. Now, quit your worrying. We're here for fun, remember? If I see Mrs. McCutcheon, I'll tell her you're looking for her."

Ina gasped. "Look! There's Heather! Oh, and Evie too! I must say hello. Are you coming, Hayden?" she said as she hurried forward.

"You go on," he said to her retreating back. "I think Morgan is waiting for me in the saloon." He stuffed his hands in his pockets and turned on his heel. He made for the alley that would take him to the back of the Hitching Post. Suffering through small talk with Heather and Evie wasn't his idea of a nice, relaxing time.

Nope. I'll go see Fancy. Her game of one hundred and one questions just might take his mind off his problems.

Chapter Thirty-Three

There were townsfolk everywhere. Heather walked along on Roady's arm as if it were the most natural thing in the world. In the gazebo, four men wearing black pants, black vests, and black hats warmed their voices by humming or singing softly. A reed-thin woman in a long black dress set a fiddle under her chin. She drew the bow across the strings several times with expertise, creating a beautiful sound. Once the bystanders heard the notes, they began to gather around, their eyes bright with anticipation.

Ina appeared and wrapped Heather in her arms. Heather couldn't help but close her eyes and melt into the woman's embrace. A hot surge of emotion prickled the backs of her eyes.

Evie smiled at the two.

"How are you, my dear?" Ina asked, smoothing back some loose hairs from Heather's face. "I've missed you."

The endearment went straight to Heather's heart. She was such a good woman who had even better intentions. Too bad her son didn't feel the same. "Very well, Ina. It's good to see you."

"Howdy, Ina," Roady said. Heather felt her face heat up when he pulled her arm closer.

Ina immediately noticed. The older woman

looked between her and Evie. "Good day, Mr. Guthrie."

He chuckled. "Now, *when* have you started calling me Mr. Guthrie, Ina? We've been friends for years."

That seemed to stymie her, as if she didn't know how to respond.

"Ina, I'm so happy Mr. Klinkner is here, too," Heather filled in. "I saw you driving into town."

"He is. He's staying in the surrey because of his leg."

Over Ina's shoulder, Francis stuck his head into the group. "Where's Hayden?"

As if feeling outnumbered, Ina stiffened. "I believe he said he was going to the saloon. Why don't you go get him, Francis? The singers almost look ready."

Francis hurried off.

Ina patted Heather's hand before Roady led her away, Evie and Chance by their side.

Heather gave Roady a speculative glance. He seemed different today. Shy. It was a change for him and she wondered at the reason.

Evie leaned in. "How is everything going with Roady?" she whispered close to Heather's ear. "He's so handsome."

She glanced at Roady to be sure he was still talking with Chance.

"What? Don't you think he's handsome?"

"Yes, but . . ."

Evie winked, making Heather do a double take. What was going on with her friend? Evie knew her heart. It would take time for her to get over Hayden. Why was she suddenly pulling for Roady?

"But what? You said the other night that you and Hayden were just friends. Has something changed?"

"No."

"If he came a-courting, what would you do?"

"Evie!" She let go of Roady's arm and took hold of Evie's shoulders, turning her away from the men. "Just what are you up to?" she said softly. "I'd really like to know."

Evie looked coyly away. "Why on earth do you think I'm up to something? I just wondered, is all."

"Because this is totally out of character for you. You know how I feel. You know I'm only walking out with Roady because, well . . ." She glanced away, not knowing how to finish her statement. "I don't know why."

"Because he's a handsome, nice fella who would make somebody a wonderful husband." Her eyebrows rose. "Correct?"

Heather nodded.

"But if you *had* to choose, I think you'd still choose Hayden."

Heather tried to object.

Evie held up her hand to silence her. "Am I correct?"

"What are you two girls whispering about?" Chance asked. "We need to get a spot on the grass."

Evie drilled Heather with a look that said, *Well?*

When Heather nodded, a smile broke out on Evie's face and she took Chance's proffered arm. "Thought so."

They headed for a nice shady area that had a good view.

Morgan was on the other side of the field. He smiled at her and waved.

Once again, Heather sent a silent prayer of thanks that he was now here in Y Knot.

The group under the gazebo launched into "Oh, My Darling Clementine."

"How long do they sing?" Heather asked.

"About an hour," Roady answered.

Francis came over and whispered something into Chance's ear.

The color in Chance's face deepened. "Tell him to go away," he responded quietly, but Heather still overheard.

"What's going on?" she asked.

"Nothing."

Before he had a chance to say more, the young farmer who had stopped Heather on the street the other day appeared. He held his hat in his hands and clearly had gussied up. "Excuse me for barging in," he began. "If you remember, my name is Tobit Preece. I was wondering if you'd had a chance to read my letter."

"Just hold up," Roady said forcefully. "Can't you see the lady is out with me? She ain't taking new prospects at this time." Roady took a threatening step in his direction. "You wait your turn."

"I've *been* waiting."

Heather remembered his vivid blue eyes and chestnut hair. He looked to be about Travis's age, and the thought of her oldest brother made her smile.

He responded with one of his own. "You didn't read it, did you?" the new suitor said, ignoring Roady.

"No. I'm sorry."

"Then I'll just have to tell you myself. I have a farm with a sturdy house. Was my grandpappy's, but I'm fixing the porch and working the pasture now. Along with breeding some livestock, I have several hundred dollars in the bank. I don't drink and I don't spend much time in saloons." He sent a pointed glance at Roady. "I'm ready to get married today. I promise I can—*and will*—make you happy. I'm asking you right now."

"Oh, my!" Evie gasped, her eyes startled wide.

Heather shook off her surprise. "I most certainly can't—"

He held up his hand. "I have more to offer you

than this cowpoke. But don't answer me right now. Think about my offer until after the concert. I'll be waiting on the boardinghouse porch."

When the young man turned to go, Roady grasped him by the shoulder. "You just can't barge in and propose to Heather! I'm the one who is supposed to—" He clamped his mouth closed.

"It's a free country, mister, and I just did." Tobit pulled his hat on and disappeared in the crowd.

The singers had finished. Everyone was listening to what had just happened.

Chance whispered something in Roady's ear.

Roady nodded, his face flamed scarlet. Without another word, Chance disappeared in the opposite direction.

Heather looked at her hands. *Oh my Lord! Roady was going to ask her to marry him. What should I do?* And what about Tobit Preece, the handsome, sincere young farmer? He was the first to propose and he wanted an answer in less than an hour.

Chapter Thirty-Four

The saloon was dead. Hayden wished Francis would go back to the gathering and leave him alone. The lad had come crashing through the saloon doors, a wild look in his eyes. Since then, Francis had been badgering him to join everyone over at the gazebo. No doing. As soon as the Twilight Singers were through, he'd pack up his parents and head home.

"Just come over for a minute, Hayden. Morgan wants to tell you something."

Hayden laughed mirthlessly. "I can tell you're lying, Francis. You just made that up. What is so all-fired important for me to come see? If it's Heather, I don't want any part of it. I can't take another rejection from her. You've all had your fun teasing me but I'm not rising to the bait." Because of the lack of customers—thanks to the performance at the gazebo—Abe sat at a table playing solitaire and Fancy wasn't to be found.

Chance came through the doors, looked quickly around, and came straight for him.

"They send out reinforcements?" Hayden muttered.

"Maybe," Chance retorted, his features hard.

Hayden shrugged and pushed some sawdust with his boot. Francis was one thing, but Chance was another. The rivalry between them felt old all of a sudden, especially since he couldn't remember what had started the trouble in the first place. When Chance leaned on the bar next to him, Hayden asked, "Can I buy you a beer then?"

"No, thanks."

"Say what you came to say."

"Actually, I don't know why I'm wasting my time. I guess this is for Evie, not you."

Hayden barked out a laugh. "Evie? How does she play into this? Are you running errands now for your wife?"

Color came up in Chance's face. He looked as if he might storm out. "She has a notion that Heather is in love with you!" Rancor sharpened his voice. "I have no idea if it's true, but I trust what she's saying. Do you have any feelings for her at all?"

Hayden forced a low, caustic laugh as a bitter swirl of emotion threatened to choke off his windpipe. "Pretty personal question, don't you think, Holcomb? When did you start playing matchmaker?"

Chance's jaw clenched hard enough to work the muscle several times.

"Hey, you two." Francis spoke up. "Ain't no call to get testy. Just come on and talk it out."

"No doing." Chance stalked to the door. He stopped, looking over the batwing doors for several moments.

Hayden turned back to the bar, feeling utterly

miserable. Nothing was ever going to feel right again. He imagined Heather cooking dinner for Roady, laughing at his corny jokes, heading off to bed.

With a curse, Chance turned and stomped back. "You just going to let Roady up and marry her without trying to stop him? Why? Because you're embarrassed how things played out in the beginning? I don't see that as being important. A month from now, only one person in Y Knot is going to give a damn who married who and why—*you!* Then before long, she'll come waltzing down the street carrying another man's baby. I wouldn't like living out my lonely days on what-ifs and if-onlys. At least I'm man enough to give it a go!"

"Why you—"

Hayden lunged and grabbed Chance by the throat.

Abe jumped up from his game and cards fluttered to the dirty wooden floor.

Francis flung himself onto Hayden's back and hung on like a tick. Abe tried to pull them apart as they wrestled against each other, strength for strength.

"Stop it!" Francis shouted. "The shindig is almost over. That farmer is going to be offering for Miss Heather's hand, and if he does, you know Roady will too. You don't have much time!"

Francis's words worked through the haze of

fury driving Hayden. He loosened his grip on Chance.

Chance pushed him away, fighting lust still plain in his eyes.

"What did you say?" he asked Francis.

"That's what I've been trying to tell you, Hayden. If you don't make a move, Heather is being proposed to today! That stranger has a lot to offer. He rattled off a list of things that would impress any woman."

Hayden turned back to his beer.

"Did you hear what he said?" Chance said to the back of his head.

"I heard. But it doesn't make a difference. Heather already turned me down. I asked her to marry me . . . she said no."

"What!" the three men said in unison. Chance and Francis gaped at Abe, making the bartender shrug and say, "Well, I didn't know that."

"Time's running out," Chance said.

Hayden looked him in the eye. "The other day, after I brought Heather out to your place, I realized I'd—" He stopped and looked pointedly at Francis.

The young man's face clouded. "I'll be waiting over here." Francis ambled a few feet away.

"I'd fallen in love with her," Hayden said quietly. "Not only that, but I wanted to marry her too. So, I wrote her a letter—just like everyone else . . ."

"And?"

"Nothing. She didn't even have the decency to tell me no to my face. Guess it's only fair after what my family put her through."

"Were you clear with your intentions?"

Hayden couldn't believe he was sharing this with Chance. "Yes. I told her I loved her," he mumbled. "I even proposed. She didn't even acknowledge it. That shows how much she thinks of me."

"No! It doesn't!" Francis had sneaked up when they were deep in conversation. "She never even read your letter!"

Hayden whipped around. "What! How do you know?"

"Because I was in the mercantile the day Miss Heather told Mr. Simpson she didn't want no more letters and for him to keep them. She had him look through and give her anything from St. Louis or Sweetwater Springs."

"Idiot." Chance straightened and poked him in the chest. "Truth be told, she's been pining over you as much as you've been pining over her."

Dispirited, Hayden shook his head. "Sorry, but I don't buy it. Just more of your matchmaking wishful thinking." He'd not let his hopes go there again. Rejection hurt too darn much. Better to suck up the pain and try to move on.

Francis bolted to the door. Stopped. Listened.

"It's over. The people are going home." He dashed out the door and was gone.

"Well, aren't you going to do anything?"

"Yeah, I'm taking my parents back to the mill." Chance just stood there, eyeing him incredulously. "I'll finally be able to show Evie what I always believed about you. A fool with no guts."

Francis crashed back through the swinging doors, his face as red as a candy apple as he gasped for breath.

"Here!" He shoved something into Hayden's face. "Take it. It's your unopened letter. If Mr. Simpson finds out I stole it, he'll have my hide."

Chapter Thirty-Five

The musicians basked in the appreciative applause of the townsfolk after the concluding number. They descended into the small crowd, talking and shaking hands. A little girl ran up and hugged the legs of the woman fiddle player until the woman bent down and picked her up.

Heather smiled when Roady looked her way.

"How'd you like it," he asked.

"Very much. Reminded me of St. Louis a little. We used to have lots of concerts. It's nice to know Y Knot has culture, too."

He patted her hand, which was still protectively wedged in the crook of his arm. "Well, a *little* culture, anyway—a *very* little. You hungry? We could get a piece of pie at the Biscuit Barrel."

Heather didn't have a smidgen of appetite. She'd watched Ina surreptitiously throughout the whole show, hoping to get a glimpse of Hayden. When the musicians had announced their last song, her anticipation had faded and died.

"Thank you, no. I had a bite just before you came for me."

He nodded. "All right. We could take a walk up the street, if you'd like. Have you seen the petrified tree we have on the east side? It's pretty spectacular. I think you'd like it."

"Actually, Roady, I'm a bit tired. All this talking and socializing has worn me out. Would you mind if we just started for the boardinghouse?"

His understanding eyes crinkled nicely at the corners. "Of course not. Won't hurt my feelings at all."

Was she that transparent? Heather could tell he knew exactly what she was about. He was a good man. A kind man. He'd make someone a wonderful husband.

Just not me.

They started toward Main Street when Tobit Preece rounded the corner from the east, and Hayden, flanked by Chance and Francis, came from the west.

Roady stiffened instantly, and then sighed deeply. "What d'ya know?" he said, pulling her closer to his side. "Seems I have some competition for your affection, Heather."

Tobit, the closest, stepped in their path first, stopping them. "I got tired of waiting and was afraid you'd spirit her off somewhere else," he said crossly to Roady. He held out a small bouquet of wildflowers he must have picked from somewhere. "Here, Miss Heather, these are for you." He handed them to Heather before Roady had a chance to object.

What is Hayden doing here? Especially now?

Hayden pulled up short, only a few feet away, a strange look in his eyes.

She wasn't interested in Tobit Preece, but it felt kind of good to show Hayden she did have a couple of sincere suitors.

Bringing the flowers to her nose, she watched Hayden from beneath her lashes. "Thank you, Mr. Preece. They're lovely." She touched one small yellow daisy with her free hand, and then smiled up at him. She hoped God would forgive her for leading Tobit on, but the look on Hayden's face was a balm to her aching heart. "This is so thoughtful."

"You're w-welcome," Tobit stammered, as if he hadn't expected to find her or for her to act receptive. "Have you thought about what I said earlier?"

Roady's expression inexplicably matched one of Lina's when she'd just cooked up a tasty treat. Satisfaction at a job well done.

She stared at him, puzzled.

Roady coughed when he saw her looking, and his expression clouded. "I don't appreciate you barging in, Preece," he said angrily. "Take back your flowers, at least until I deliver her home."

"No doing. They're hers now."

Chance nudged Hayden, who still stood a few feet away. Hayden looked uncertain, as if he had something he wanted to say but was holding back. A lock of his sandy hair fell over his forehead, making her hands itch to push it back into place—and caress his face while she was at it. His powerful arms and chest, covered by a soft-looking red plaid shirt, hugged his body, making hers react.

No!

Roady stepped forward, taking her with him. "Well, we'll be going now." He dipped his head to Chance as they left a speechless Mr. Preece to watch them go.

"Hey!" Preece started to object.

Morgan appeared from nowhere. He clamped his hand on the newcomer's shoulder and whispered into his ear. Right then, a red-faced Mr. Simpson came limping down the boardwalk as fast as he could go. Townspeople stopped on the street to gawk.

"Francis! I saw you steal that letter. You return it right now!" he hollered. "Stealing mail is a federal crime."

Evie, followed by Ina, Lucky, and June, hurried over to Chance and Hayden to see what was happening. Mr. Simpson, breathless and shaky, had to be bolstered up by Chance.

"What in tarnation is going on? More trouble?" Jack Jones asked, riding up in the street. He dismounted and came forward, reins in hand.

Mr. Simpson pointed at Francis, still puffing hard. "I was just sweeping up when this rascal barged into the store and went straight behind the mail counter where I keep the mail. He rifled through some letters addressed to Miss Stanford, then bolted out the door with one. Arrest him, Deputy. He broke the law."

Francis looked around in a panic.

"Go on, Francis," Roady said. "Put out your hands so the deputy can arrest you. McCutcheons don't want some thief working for 'em."

"B-But," he sputtered. "But—"

"Roady's right, Francis," Luke McCutcheon said, just now showing up to the group. A pretty woman with a worried expression clung to one arm. He jiggled a baby in the other. Several children followed the couple. "Let the man cuff you." A corner of his mouth quirked. "Maybe this time you'll learn."

Mr. Simpson winked at Roady, as if pleased with his performance. In that moment, Hayden knew he'd been had. He had a decision to make. He could either be angry at his friends for interfering and stomp away fuming. That childish behavior would probably make him lose his opportunity with Heather forever. Especially if this yahoo, Preece, had caught her attention this afternoon.

Or, he could do what his heart wanted him to do. Put an end to this madness by falling to one knee and spilling his guts, after which he'd let the cards fall where they may. If she turned him down, then at least he wouldn't be living his life with regrets, as Chance had said. Option two was his only *real* choice.

Chance nudged him again, hard this time. "You gonna let the deputy lock up Francis when the boy was just trying to help you?"

Time's up.

Heather's attention was riveted on him, waiting for his answer, as was everyone else's.

"Guess I can't do that, Chance. Jack," he said, addressing the confused-looking deputy. Seemed Jack wasn't in on the joke. "Francis was only doing what I'd asked him to do by retrieving a letter I'd written to Miss Stanford." He held the letter up.

Heather's gaze locked with his.

A murmur of excited voices started on one side of the group and flowed to the other.

Hayden almost smiled. He went forward, feeling as if he were in a dream. He gave it to her with a shaky hand. For a moment he thought Tobit might try to intervene, but Morgan's trusty presence behind the man calmed his fears.

"What's this?" She spoke so softly that he had a hard time hearing her.

"A letter. I wrote it the night after we went out to the Holcombs'. Seems you never got it."

He'd never heard the town so quiet. From the corner of his vision, he saw his mother standing next to Evie, leaning forward with the rest of them, straining to hear their conversation.

Sorrow and so much more flitted across Heather's face. "No."

"Will you read it now?"

She glanced at the post in her hands. Slowly she handed her flowers to him. The envelope quivered. She worked to get it open, and he wasn't sure if she was embarrassed or if her insides were quaking like his out of excitement and fear.

Hayden kept his gaze anchored on Heather's face, needing to gauge her reaction to his words.

"What are they doing, Mommy?" The little girl's voice floated up from somewhere in the crowd, starting a soft ripple of laughter.

Hayden felt a glimmer of hope fixing him to this day, this moment.

"Shhh, sugar," Fancy's sultry voice purred from the back. "This is the best part."

Heather looked up from reading, tears welling in her eyes. "Are you sure?"

"About what? That I love you? Or that I want to make you my wife?" Before she could answer, he pulled Heather into his arms and kissed her for all he was worth.

Heather's arms wrapped around his shoulders and she pulled him close.

All the nights lying awake imagining what it would feel like couldn't hold a candle to the real thing. *Nothing* compared. Heather in his arms was heaven on earth. If only they were alone, he'd give her a thousand kisses, and show her just how much he loved her, needed her. But with everyone standing close, one kiss would have to satisfy for now. "Well?" he asked, his lips still close to hers.

"I love you, Hayden. It's only been you from the start."

A cheer went up from all around. He even thought he saw Preece cheering along with the rest of them.

He picked up Heather and twirled her around.

She squealed, then laughed.

When Hayden set her down, he had one more question for her. "What about all the letters you've received? What are you going to do with them? Don't you want to read them, you know, so you can be sure?"

Her eyes twinkled merrily.

He had no idea what she'd reply.

"Those? I haven't read one of them yet and I'm not planning to." She leaned in. "I think they'll make wonderful fire starters when the snow starts to fall," she whispered. "What do you think?"

In a haze of euphoria, he pulled Heather close so he could speak into her ear. "If you want. But I don't think we'll need much help getting a fire started, darlin'. None at all."

Chapter Thirty-Six

That Sunday, after the church service, Reverend Crittlestick married Hayden and Heather in a simple service. Pretty much everyone showed up, eager to see the two wed—the town's own private fairy tale. Heather, beaming radiantly on Hayden's arm, waited at the top of the stairs of the little blue church for Francis to bring the surrey around. Excitement swirled around inside her.

"Look." She laughed at the sight of the gussied-up conveyance. Ribbons and bows adorned Fritz and Stonewall's manes and tails, and streamers fluttered from the canopy. A large sign attached to the bumper read JUST MARRIED—FINALLY!

Hayden straightened. "Hey, those are mine." He pointed to a pair of boots dragging behind the surrey on several lengths of rope, along with a couple of tin cans. "Francis?"

"Sorry." The young man didn't look at all regretful.

"He'll get 'em cleaned up," Lucky promised. "Don't be a-worrying. Francis is a darn fine polisher."

Stef Hannessy, owner of the Night Owl Mine, let out a hearty chortle. "I have a pair that needs a good buffing if he runs out of things to do. Tomorrow when you come out with the next load of lumber, Hayden, I'll send 'em home with you to give to Francis."

Heather laughed.

Francis, waiting in the driver's seat, ducked his head. "Morgan said it was all right if I used 'em."

"Don't go blaming that on me, kid." Morgan looked down at June, who smiled up into his face. She was still dressed in her jeans, vest, and hat, but looked mighty feminine all the same. Weddings must bring out her soft side, Heather thought. Or maybe it's Morgan.

"What are you smiling about?" Hayden picked up her hand and placed a kiss on the back of it.

"Just a little something I'm thinking about Morgan and June."

He followed her gaze and made a low approving sound in his throat.

Jack Jones strode toward the church and stopped at the bottom of the step. He doffed his hat to Heather. "I have some important news."

Hayden frowned. "Can't it wait? This is our wedding day."

"Sorry, it can't. I just got a telegram from the sheriff over in Pine Grove. Seems your steam engine had a little help blowing up."

Everyone grew quiet.

"Was it Abner Lundgren?" Hayden asked, shaking his head. "My pa could have been killed.

He had motive, losing the Night Owl bid to us like he did."

"No, not Lundgren. He didn't have anything to do with it. It was his wife. Seems she didn't like losing all that money and hired that traveling salesman who comes through town every few months to do something about it. He had one too many whiskeys and was grumbling in the saloon about not getting paid for his services. Both have been arrested."

Astonished whispers floated through the townspeople.

"Thank God it wasn't Abner," Stef Hannessy boomed. "I wouldn't like to think he'd sink that low. But I sure believe it about his spiteful wife."

Evie pressed in close. "Heather, don't let this news ruin your wedding day. I'm so happy for you and Hayden. You make the perfect couple. I knew from the moment I saw the two of you together and he gave you 'the look.' Are you excited about tonight? Don't be nervous. Or scared."

Hayden, now free of the deputy, looked around Heather to Evie. "What are you two whispering about? Must be naughty because both your faces are pinked up." He leaned in and kissed Heather on the lips. "I don't mind if you're talking about me."

Heather gasped that he was so close to the truth. "Hayden!"

Chance came up the stairs. "Mmm. What's that smell? Someone must be frying chicken—in lots of hot oil."

Evie's face turned three shades of green. "Chance?"

"Oh, no!" Pushing past Hayden, Chance scooped Evie up in his arms and bolted down the steps two at a time. "Let us through, let us through," he called as he went, and everyone stepped back, creating a path.

"Looks like there's gonna be a little Holcomb to contend with come spring." Luke tipped his hat back and a grin split his face. "Let me know if you need any pointers, Chance," he called at Chance's retreating back, making everyone laugh, including Faith. "I've had enough experience to open a school for fathers-to-be."

Hayden leaned in close. "Well, darlin', it's time to go. You ready?"

Heather nodded, feeling like the luckiest woman in the world. Hayden took her hand and they descended the steps to a shower of rice, laughter, and love.

"Good luck!"

"Congratulations!"

"*Prost!*" Mr. Lichtenstein called. The kindly merchant's lips wobbled and his face clouded over. Mr. Herrick handed him a hanky and the German dabbed at his eyes.

Heather couldn't miss Ina and Norman on

the outside of the crowd, him on his crutches as tears ran down Ina's face. "Look, Hayden, your mother, she's so sweet." A look of sadness crossed Hayden's eyes before he nodded. But then a chuckle chased away the wistful expression, much to Heather's relief.

"Yes, I think she's the happiest of all—except for me, of course," he said quickly. "I hope we can fill the house with lots of happy little children as soon as possible."

Laughing and ducking the rice amid all the excitement, Hayden handed her up into the backseat of the surrey.

"I'll do my best to fulfill your wish," she whispered into his ear when he climbed in.

"I'll hold you to that, darlin'. You can bet on it."

As Francis flicked the reins and the surrey jerked forward, Casper Slack, atop his ancient mule—also decorated for the occasion—clucked loudly to his mount and started to strum.

> *Heather and Hayden got married one day;*
> *Hayden was star-eyed and tongue-tied they say;*
> *Sweet Heather was dressed up in ribbons and rings;*
> *Says Hayden, "You angel, where are your wings?"*

Acknowledgments

Creating "the mail-order brides books" has been a joy from the first paragraph. Heather's story, like Evie's, just seemed to spill out, writing itself. That said, I couldn't have delivered the finished product without the help of more than a few hardworking professionals and loyal friends, plus the love and support of my family.

My thanks go to Debra Holland, my other half in the "the mail-order" series. To Leslie Lynch and Sandy Loyd, for not holding back while critiquing the first or second draft. To Jennifer Forsberg Meyer for the in-depth developmental help and editing. And to my fantastic beta reading team, for their sharp eyes, dedication, and enthusiasm: Mildred Robles, Kandice Hutton, Lorna Samboceti Wren, and Rose Reiter. I appreciate you all so much!

And, as always, heartfelt thanks go to my delightful readers, who want an adventure bursting with love and romance—as well as a good horse, a gunfight now and then, and lots of slow cowboy charm. You've filled my life with happiness!

About the Author

Caroline Fyffe was born in Waco, Texas, the first of many towns she would call home during her father's career with the US Air Force. A horse aficionado from an early age, she earned a Bachelor of Arts in communications from California State University-Chico before launching what would become a twenty-year career as an equine photographer. She began writing fiction to pass the time during long days in the show arena, channeling her love of horses and the Old West into a series of Western historicals. Her debut novel, *Where the Wind Blows*, won the Romance Writers of America's prestigious Golden Heart Award as well as the Wisconsin RWA's Write Touch Readers' Award. She and her husband have two grown sons and live in the Pacific Northwest.

Want news on releases, giveaways, and bonus reads? Sign up for Caroline's newsletter at:
www.carolinefyffe.com

See her Equine Photography:
www.carolinefyffephoto.com

LIKE her Facebook Author Page:
Facebook.com/CarolineFyffe
Please join my Facebook Readers Group—
We're waiting for YOU!

Twitter: @carolinefyffe

Write to her at: caroline@carolinefyffe.com

Center Point Large Print
600 Brooks Road / PO Box 1
Thorndike, ME 04986-0001 USA

(207) 568-3717

US & Canada:
1 800 929-9108
www.centerpointlargeprint.com